AN ORPHAN FOR THE DUKE

A HISTORICAL REGENCY ROMANCE

AUDREY ASHWOOD

An Orphan for the Duke

(Large Print Edition V3)

Copyright © 2020 Audrey Ashwood

Print ISBN: 9798632901741

ABOUT THIS NOVEL

A broken duke.
An unexpected arrival.
Can her presence heal the man who swore
never to love again?

Seven years ago, the Duke of Devonshire's
heart was shattered. After his late-wife's death,
the duke immersed himself in work and duty
so he could numb the pain. Despite his possession of immense wealth, a historic title, strik-
ingly handsome looks, and not few possible

prospects, he wants for nothing in this world – except to be left alone.

That solitude ends suddenly with the arrival of a desperate letter from an old friend, containing his dying wish that the duke care for his daughter. The duke, unable to ignore his dying friend's appeal, orders the house to be prepared for the child's arrival – much-loved toys and dolls, a room with the best views in the front of the house, and a swing in the garden. Only a few days later, Isabella arrives at the luxurious Hardwick Manor.

She is a shock to the duke – in both age and appearance. He was expecting a child, and not a stunningly beautiful woman!

What fate awaits the woman who has lost everything? What of the duke who has sworn never to love again?

ummer 1783
Derbyshire, England

MATTHEW WALKED along the narrow dirt road at the river's edge. His feet were aching. His stomach grumbled. His throat was parched from thirst, but he was not going to give up. Not yet. At the tender age of seven, he was a determined boy. His tutors called him stubborn, which he considered to be a compliment. That same stubbornness was what had led him to sneak away from his home after breakfast, and which would not permit him to return until he was successful in his quest. *His quest* – yes, that was how he described his current adventure. He was a knight on a quest, just like the stories his tutors made him read about knights of old – jousting and fighting dragons.

However, for him, there was not a dragon, neither young nor old, nor a field of honour to prove his mettle. No, his quest was a simple one, but it was one he still considered to be equally as important as slaying a dragon to save a princess. There was not a princess, either, only the young Miss Georgiana – a girl who was near his own age and beautiful as a rose, or so he thought, and he blushed just thinking of her. Her face was as lovely as any he had beheld in paintings. She possessed blonde curls which she wore in ringlets, much as the angels he had observed in the stained-glass windows of the village church. That most certainly made her the prettiest girl he had ever laid eyes on. She was the epitome of everything he held dear, and more than that, he also considered her his closest friend.

She and her father lived nearby and would often come by carriage to pay a call on his father. Yesterday afternoon at tea was the same as usual, with one exception: Georgiana had been utterly devastated. Her sadness came from the loss of her puppy, a dog she adored. She feared it was lost and hungry, after it slipped away on a stroll the day before. The puppy had bounded after a rabbit in the garden and had become lost after chasing the hapless rabbit out of the open gate.

Ever since Matthew had heard of the puppy's disappearance, he had been relentlessly searching the grounds of his father's estate. He reasoned that if Georgiana and her family lived not more than a short carriage ride away, it was quite possible that the puppy may have come onto the estate. As Matthew well knew from his personal experience of his father's packs of prize-winning hounds, dogs did not care much for borders, fences, or walls, *if* there was a way around. He also knew that dogs were fast runners and could easily traverse a great distance, on occasion matching and surpassing the speed of horses.

Armed with his knowledge of dogs and his willingness to search the entire estate if it should prove necessary, his search (or, better, his quest) began as he and Georgiana searched the garden, then the stables. When Georgiana left, he continued to look for the lost dog after dinner, and into the late hours – long after he was supposed to be in bed. Following his thorough search of the buildings on the estate, which were a shelter he presumed any puppy would find welcoming, he became convinced that the animal must have wondered into the woods. *If he was a puppy, it was where he might go,* he thought, *to run after rabbits and deer, enjoying the unbridled freedom of being a dog in the forest.*

With that idea and his absolute confidence that he had as good a chance as anyone else of finding the lost dog, maybe even better, he set out after breakfast the next day, with little care for his own comfort. He smiled. Surely, there would be a reward. Not a monetary one – he had no care for money. There would be the lovely Georgiana's heartfelt gratitude. She was his lady fair and he would be her knight – but first, he had to prove himself to her. What better way than to return her beloved pet to her tearful thanks, and maybe a small token of her affection. A lock of her golden hair would be enough, but he dared not hope. Not yet. The sun was overhead, he was starving, and there was not a single sign of the dog in his corner of Derbyshire. Yet, Matthew was stubborn. He refused to accept failure, and so he continued his search.

Despite his absolute belief in his own ability to find the dog, the hours without rest or food were beginning to take their toll. The day was warm, and the sun continued to shine down through the trees with its relentless brightness. It was especially hot for this time of year. Summer had always been pleasant for a boy his age, with riding and other similar outdoor pursuits, but he could never recall being as thirsty as he was on this particular day. He barely recalled his last sip of something wet – it had been at breakfast, many hours ago. His lips were dry, and he was beginning to weaken. But, he would not return home empty-handed, no matter the consequences – even if he met his doom by thirsting to death under the scorching summer sun.

He gazed at the river. The swiftly flowing stream carried over the rocks with a quick pace, and with a sound that beckoned to him as sirens calling from the watery depths. He decided that he could afford a drink, despite having been warned time and time again by his father and his tutors to avoid the river because of its swift current. A current, it was said, that could be treacherous to a child of his age who did not know how to swim.

He shrugged away the memories of all the warnings he had received about the river. He decided that leaning down from the bank to drink the water would not harm him. How could there be any danger of drowning if all he did was drink? Leaving the road, he made his way to the riverbank. He could practically taste the delicious cool water running down his dry throat as he ignored the slippery mud at the river's edge.

He leaned down on his knees, cupped his hand, and reached into the rushing water. As he was raising the water to his parched lips, he heard a sound that was as desperate and heart-wrenching as any noise he had ever encountered. Not far from where he was crouched, he heard a plaintive whining, low and barely audible above the sound of the breeze blowing through the trees and the tall grasses on the banks – but nonetheless, he heard it near the water. He listened, startled by what sounded like crying – *or was it whining?* – it was so soft.

He looked around frantically as he jumped to his feet. Searching the water, looking for the source of such a pitiable noise, he suddenly spotted a furry bundle floating and struggling in the current not far from him. The bundle – it appeared to be a pile of rags or fur – was small, brown, and fighting to find a way onto a nearby rock. The rock was too slick and the current too strong, and it whined again woefully, before becoming submerged in the relentless water. To his horror, he realised that this bundle, this ragged scrap of fur must be the puppy, and it was drowning before his eyes!

Without a thought of his own safety or the dangers of the river, he jumped into the water. The river was not so deep near the bank, and the dog was not too far. With a few steps, he could reach the animal before it succumbed. Stepping farther into the river, he felt the current pulling at him, and it forced him to struggle to keep his balance in the soft mud that sucked at his shoes and feet. The puppy was fighting, trying to raise its head above the water as Matthew fought with all his might to reach it. He willed himself farther, until the water was up to his shoulders and tried not to think of how hard it was becoming to keep from being swept away. He was too close to the puppy to worry about that now.

He reached the puppy, grasped the wiggling animal with both hands, and thrust it out of the water with all his might, while the animal sputtered and shook from fear. The water was deeper here. It was nearly up to his neck, and as he held the puppy out of the current, it became increasingly obvious that he may need saving himself. Matthew, being the determined and courageous sort of boy he was, did not succumb to the rising panic that threatened to engulf him. Instead, he searched for any means of escape or assistance, and saw a rock nearby, the river swirling around it. If he could manage to get the puppy to the rock, he may find a way to retrieve the poor beast later. At least, he decided the puppy would be out of the river, while he waded closer to the shore.

Although the puppy was a wriggling mass of fur, terrified and whimpering, it did not have much fight left in its little body. Matthew had no way of knowing how long the poor beast had struggled in the river, but it was alive, and that was all that mattered. Moving against the current to reach the rock took all of his strength, but he was valiant, as any knight three times his age would be. As he thrust the dog onto the rock, he prayed the puppy would not slip back into the water.

Matthew realised it far too late.

He was in trouble.

He lost his footing in the muck of the riverbed and his head went under the water. He fought to stand, as his lungs filled with water. He sputtered and coughed. He tried to regain his footing and return to the safety of the shore. He had made a terrible error, but how could he have foreseen it?

His head went under once more. This time, there was no regaining his footing as the submerged hole was deeper than he was tall. Fighting to survive with all of his energy, he willed himself to rise to the surface, waving his arms and kicking, which used all of his strength. He tried to gasp for air, but more water rushed into his mouth. His muscles ached. He could not breathe. He feared that he would never see the surface. All around him was the mighty, rushing water. When he began to succumb to fear, he prayed that God would save him. He uttered a silent prayer in his head as the panic, he swore not to feel, engulfed him like the waters of the river.

This was the end. This was how he would meet his doom.

Perhaps Georgiana, oh, his sweet Georgiana... would think of him as brave for giving his life to save her dog. He wished he... could be anywhere but... under the... waters...

He was seized by darkness.

From above – he knew not how – he felt himself being pulled from the current. Suddenly his head was above the water as he coughed and tried to see what was happening. His eyes were blurry from being submerged. His heart was thundering in his ears, and he could barely breathe. Somewhere he heard a dog whining and barking.

Matthew was vaguely aware that he was being dragged out of the river.

A short time later, he lay on the bank. He wiped his eyes and saw the shadowy figure of a man – *or was it a boy?* – in the river, reaching the puppy and bringing it ashore.

Matthew felt a dry handkerchief thrust into his hand. Instinctively, he wiped his face and eyes with it before turning over onto his stomach. His arms were shaking as he raised himself while he coughed up water. His lungs were burning, his stomach heaved, and his body ached. Yet, as he coughed up the river water, he realised that he was alive. What's more, the puppy was alive, too, and it licked him in exhausted gratitude. Gripping the now-soiled-and-damp handkerchief, he looked at the person who had saved him. His sight was no longer blurry. The person was not a man, but was not his age, either. It was a boy, but one who was older than Matthew's seven years.

The boy sat down beside Matthew, and the puppy crawled over to him. Despite the dog's exhausted state, its eyes were shining with adoration as it gazed at his companion. With a shake of his wet fur, his tail began to wag slowly. Matthew looked closely at the boy, saw his dark hair was wet against his face, his breeches torn at the knee, and rivulets of blood were staining the fabric from a wound.

The boy investigated the tear and his injury and shrugged. "That must have happened when I dove in. A rock is to blame, I wager."

Matthew nodded his head, as the boy continued, "The name is John Thornton," he said brightly, offering his hand to Matthew.

"Matthew Danvers," Matthew said, reaching out his hand to shake John's.

"I know who you are," John answered, a bemused expression on his face. "My father is the Earl of Chatham. He is meeting with your father today on business. I saw you jump into the river after the puppy and thought you might need help."

Matthew did not answer. Part of him was ashamed that he had almost drowned. He was not sure if he liked the fact that he had needed help, but he was grateful to John for helping him. John did not wait for an answer but smiled and winked at him. The two boys sat on the riverbank for a little while longer, letting their clothes dry out.

"What's your dog's name?" The older boy interrupted the silence while he rubbed the wet fur on top of the puppy's head.

"This dog? It does not belong to me. It belongs to Georgiana."

John snorted. "Georgiana? No wonder you were willing to risk your life to save it."

"I would have saved it even if it wasn't her dog," Matthew replied. "I like dogs."

"I like dogs, too." John nodded his head. "I would not have let it drown no more than you would. You must be very brave to have gone into the water after the animal. The current is strong. I am astonished that you had the strength to withstand it."

Beaming at the complement from the older boy, Matthew felt the sting of needing help lessen. John had called him brave. Brave, just like a knight.

Few children came to the estate, even in the company of their parents. John was different. *Yes*, thought Matthew, this was just the sort of boy he wished could be his friend; and so, he decided John could be his friend – and why not? He *was* a brave knight, after all. He had succeeded in his quest, with the aid of this fellow knight. Were they not brothers in arms as told in the stories of old? Were they not bonded by the danger they had shared in the trial?

As Matthew played with the puppy (who was now showing remarkable resilience after their near drowning), and with as much stern-ness as he could muster, Matthew knew what he had to do. It was the only proper thing for a boy in his position to do at such a moment.

He held his head as high as he was able and said in his most adult sounding tone, "John Thornton. You have saved my life and the life of this dog. I owe you a debt. You say what you want, and it will be yours as long as I can find the money for it. Well… I will have to ask my father, but he always says yes. You have my word as a Danvers… and a knight."

Matthew waited for John to say something in response that was suitable. The older boy looked at him as though he was studying him, "You are a knight? And I thought you were the son of a duke. That is the reason that you possess such admirable courage. You are a nobleman *and* a great warrior. I am honoured to be in your company." He laughed.

Matthew did not think John was mocking, as adults were sometimes prone to do. He *was* the only son of the Duke of Devonshire and the heir to the title. He was accustomed to a certain level of being pandered to, even at his young age. John Thornton, who was older than him (and much taller), did not act as if he was patronizing Matthew but seemed genuinely honoured to be his friend. It was an honour that Matthew was thrilled to bestow.

"Young Sir, since you are a knight," John

continued, "it would not do for anyone to think that you nearly drowned, or me, for that matter. Our fathers might be anxious if they thought that we were in danger this afternoon. I would not enjoy having my freedom or yours taken away, especially as I will be staying at your house for several days, and there are surely more adventures awaiting us. If I may make a suggestion? Why don't we *not* tell anyone what really happened? You can take the credit for saving the dog, who we will say slipped into the water. We fell in trying to save the creature, which you did without my help. You will be the hero of the hour, and I will be your loyal friend."

Matthew smiled. He liked the idea – to a large extent – that he would be the hero, to be honest. In a way he was. They were both brave, but he knew better than John what an anxious father and a nervous mother could do to a boy's freedoms. If his father forbade him from leaving the house, or his mother forced him to promise not to venture out, what fun could be had that summer? Especially now that he had a new companion for riding and games!

As with any young boy of his age, he snuggled the puppy to his chest, and glanced admiringly at the older boy sitting next to him, wondering at his luck in finding more than a friend – he had found a brother.

CHAPTER 1

Thirty-six years later

HIS GRACE, the Fifth Duke of Devonshire, sat in his study at Hardwick Manor. The view from the room was spectacular. From his high-backed chair, he looked out onto a vast expanse of lawn that was designed by one of the leading landscape architects of the last century. Long narrow pools of water stretched away from the house, each one with a magnificent fountain as its focal point. Two tree-lined roads led to the grand, colonnaded entrance to his stately home – they ran along the side of the pools, creating an impressive vista from his study, the drawing room, and several of the guest rooms on the second and third floors. Greek statues, follies, and copies of temples were tucked into the garden that encircled the house, creating the impression that the house – a stunning Georgian renovation of his family's Tudor manor house – was a palace, which, in a way, it was. The home sat on sloping hills, nestled against the backdrop of the Derbyshire dales, creating a setting that looked as if it should have been the residence of royalty.

Matthew Danvers was not royalty. However, his title of Duke put him quite close to the princes and princesses of the blood of the royal family. Nevertheless, the title was inescapable, and there were days when he felt the full weight of it and the responsibilities that came with it. Being the next Duke of Devonshire and knowing it was his fate, since as early as he could recall, had made his childhood rather less innocent. From the moment he was able to walk and talk, he prepared to assume the responsibilities that came with the title of "Duke" and the property it required to be managed. Property which extended far beyond the view he now joylessly gazed upon. From Yorkshire to Kent, he had inherited several houses, all of them grand but none as magnificent as Hardwick Manor – and none as dear. This close connection had made him a frequent guest at court when he was a younger man. Now, at the age of forty-three, the view from his family's house, in his possession as the sole male heir, did nothing to cheer him. Nor did it alleviate the sadness that tinged the memory of the boyhood he had spent on the estate in the company of his dearest friend, John Thornton.

As he unfolded the letter, he recalled the summers that they had spent riding along the hillsides, and fishing in the same river that had nearly cost them their lives. They had been inseparable. John acted like an older brother, doling out advice and listening carefully to the opinions of Matthew, who was quite mature for his young years. The cherished memories of his close friend, John, flickered in his mind, as well as the event by the river that had started their friendship. *How quickly the years had passed*, he thought to himself as he read the letter clutched in his hand.

My Friend,

By the time this letter reaches you, I will have passed from this world to the next.

Do not grieve too deeply for me, my friend. I join those we have loved, but who left us so suddenly. Such is the way of life. We are all one illness or accident away from the next world. I do not fear death, rather I welcome it. In truth, I have been tired for too long now. We both know what has kept me in the land of the living for so very long, and it is out of that same desperation for the living that I write to you.

I must call in the favour you were so generous to offer so long ago. It concerns my daughter, Isabella. She is still a child, so young and innocent of the horrors of this world. Please, brother, take my darling girl and care for her. Do right by her and protect her as best as you can.

This is my deathbed wish, and the last favour I can ask of you.

Goodbye, my true and dearest friend, and brother,

John Thornton, Earl of Chatham

THE DUKE FOLDED the paper neatly and precisely and slipped it into the pocket of his coat. John was dead. Matthew had known it, even before he read those terrible words. His friend had been in poor health for many months. He had received a hastily scribbled note from John, it seemed but several years ago, a note that should have spurred Matthew into action. He had planned to travel to Norfolk to visit John and his new, second wife, but somehow, there had always been some other obligation to fulfil, some responsibility which made the journey impossible. He was horrified now to think that his dear friend, who had once been as close as a brother, had brought a daughter into the world without his even realising it. In truth, Matthew foolishly presumed that his friend John had not aged or grown weak with illness. It was just too horrible to think that the young man who had saved his life that summer's day, over thirty years ago had become sick. Perhaps it was the dark thought, the spectre of death that kept Matthew from visiting? Was it perhaps the guilt of the too many long years that had come between them?

His gaze returned to the magnificent view, but his thoughts were somewhere else. How had he managed to let the years come and go so quickly without anything more than a rare letter or a missive exchanged between him and his old friend? John had inherited the title of Earl of Chatham, and Matthew had become a Duke. Was it that there was simply so much to be done by each of them that they had grown apart? He knew that they had each become consumed by their responsibilities, each in his own world, as they assumed the mantles of their fathers: Matthew in Derbyshire and John drifting from his family's holding in the Americas, and then to the Indies before returning to England permanently.

How easy it was for Matthew to blame the distance and the weight and breadth of his duties for his not being as diligent a friend as he might have been. If John had not been abroad, if Matthew had not been entrusted and consumed with the management of several enormous estates, any number of them a Herculean task in itself. Yet, despite the distance and the years they had lost, he had not lost respect for John or changed his opinion of him.

There was no question that he would see to the matter personally. It was the least he could do for John. Could he raise John's child – his friend's *darling girl*? He struggled to recall any further details of John's second marriage, but he could not. *How old could she possibly be,* he wondered. Six years? Eight? Twelve years old at the most, he supposed. He smiled at the thought of the sound of a child's laughter in the vast rooms of his house. How cheering it would be to hear a little girl gaily singing or practicing the piano in the music room, much as his wife and his sister had done many years before.

His thoughts darkened. He had hoped that he might have a child one day, but his dear wife, Georgiana, had died unexpectedly. Unlike his dear friend, he had not remarried. Her death had left behind an uncertain future for the estate, but, far worse, it had left him grieving. That grief reminded him that love, like life, was not lasting. The smile that he had worn for a brief moment as he thought of the little girl vanished. Reading the news of his friend's death had resurrected the old hurt he had felt at Georgiana's loss… his lovely Georgiana with the golden-blonde hair.

When he thought of his dearly departed wife, he felt the dull familiar ache in his chest.

He had adored his wife from the time they were children; he still loved none but her. Could he spare any feelings for this child, Isabella? He knew he would fulfil his obligation to John, but did she not have the right to be adored, even loved? His mother would dote on her, he was sure of that, and so would his younger sister. But how could he find it in his heart to offer her any emotion now that he had lost his dear wife? Surely, if she was still alive, Georgiana would have accepted that he was fulfilling an obligation and she would be satisfied, but how was he supposed to care for the little girl when he had felt nothing in years?

He had made his decision and he admitted, however painfully, that he probably might never be able to love the child. Perhaps one day, he would be able to change that and could dote on her as he knew his own wife would have, but in his heart, he doubted that day would ever come. After all, he reasoned, accepting the child into his home would be enough. It *had* to be. If John's dying wish was to entrust his young daughter to the duke's care, he would not deny it. He owed John a debt that was more than money could repay. He owed John for every day of the past thirty-six years. If raising John's child was an opportunity to repay that debt, the duke was prepared to see that Isabella was given the best care befitting the daughter of an earl and the ward of a duke. As soon as the child was old enough, she would have the best governesses, the most accomplished music tutors for dance and art, and all manner of education befitting a child who would one day be presented at court. With the finest dresses, food, and education that money could buy, and his mother and sister doing the rest, she would surely not notice that he was unable to love her as her father once had.

He returned to his desk and quickly wrote a letter to his solicitor in London. Arrangements would have to be made if he were to accept responsibility for John's daughter. As he penned the missive, he wondered about John's other, elder child – the son of his first marriage, and therefore Isabella's half-brother. John's first wife had tragically died giving birth to her son, the duke knew that much. He speculated about what could have happened to prompt John to plead with *him* to see to his daughter. He was curious about the circumstances surrounding the whole affair, and also wondered about the son, who was heir to the Chatham title. Still, he did not wish to waste a moment on that matter any longer, not when there was a child orphaned by her mother's and father's death.

He rang for his footman and asked for the letter to be dispatched to his solicitor, Mr Hayworth, with the order that it be delivered in haste. After the letter was sent, he prepared to announce the news of his ward to his mother and sister. Without a doubt, they would be welcoming to the child – as welcoming as he hoped he could be, when she eventually arrived.

He was struck by the cold chill of a dreadfully dismal thought. It occurred to him that even with the prospect of music and laughter ringing through the house, Isabella Thornton would be more than a debt that had been repaid – in his eyes, she would be a living reminder that his friend John, and his own beloved wife, were dead.

CHAPTER 2

On the afternoon, following the news of John's death, and shortly after the reply had been sent to his solicitor, the duke left his study. He had delayed his afternoon ride on his favourite steed, a horse he enjoyed galloping across the hills, and instead he entered the drawing room. He braced himself for the reaction that he was about to receive in response to his news, and the barrage of questions that would surely follow.

The duke had complete autonomy over his family, his property, and his servants, so it was not carelessness that had preceded his unilateral decision concerning John's daughter. It was his right, and, indeed, his habit not to seek the opinions of others if he did not see an absolute necessity to consult them. In the matter of John's child, he had not consulted his mother or his sister about assuming responsibility for a ward. Nevertheless, he fully planned to enlist their help in the matter of the child's care, as befit the role of women.

He entered the room that was generally presumed to be the haven and domain of the women of his family, without remorse or anxiety. The drawing room was for teas and social occasions – events he resigned himself to attending, but which he found to be tedious, even at the best of times. The drawing room at Hardwick Manor was special. As he strode across the carpeted floor, his gaze fell upon his surroundings, which were commonplace to him, but which were designed to be viewed with awe by the guests of Hardwick Manor. With murals painted on the walls, sumptuous furnishing, and gilt and crystal objects glittering in the candlelight, the room really was quite impressive.

It was also the domain of Matthew's mother, Margaret Danvers, Her Grace, the Dowager Duchess of Devonshire, and his younger sister, Lady Diana Danvers. Whenever they were in residence, the two women held court in the drawing room, welcoming their acquaintances to the stately manor. This happened frequently, as the house functioned not only as the seat of the title and the family but as a favourite residence. When Matthew had married, his mother had moved into a smaller but still luxurious house on the grounds that her late husband had left her, along with a generous stipend, but since he had become a widower, she had begun to spend much more time in the main house. Once again, she played the part of hostess, a position that he was grateful she had undertaken.

His mother and his sister were unaccompanied by guests that afternoon, and the duke was pleased that this conversation would be finished in time for dinner. He did not wish to be delayed over this obligation any longer than necessary, not when the child had yet to arrive. Without a smile on his face or any indication that he was anticipating the arrival of a young girl to his house, the duke explained the contents of John's letter and laid out his dying wish to his mother and sister. The news was met as he had expected.

His mother completely ignored the matter of the child and quickly addressed a subject that she never ceased to mention at every opportunity.

"I do wish you would see reason that you *must* marry again," she declared after he had settled into a high-backed chair by the fireside.

His mother was a formidable woman and had always been – it was something that had not changed with her advancing years. With her lustrous grey hair pinned and curled under a lace cap and her dress of imported silk, bejewelled and trimmed with every manner of expensive embellishment, she appeared less as a duchess and more of an empress. She sat straight and perfectly poised in her chair and narrowed her eyes at her son. The duchess did not give an inch in the old argument that had been going on for some time now.

"Mother, this is not the time to discuss my prospects for matrimony. We must plan for the arrival of John's daughter, Isabella." He steered the conversation back to the matter at hand.

"All the more reason to marry again," his mother stated decisively, "to offer the poor child a mother's care, as you cannot," she finished, *rather smugly*, he thought. It was a well-worn subject where each felt they held the higher ground, and recently, he had begun to feel that it was like a series of minor skirmishes, where each had their side to fight, but where no real progress was being made.

"What a delightful proposition, to have a child with us here at Hardwick Manor!" his sister chimed in, smiling broadly.

Her role was meant to be that of an arbiter, Matthew thought to himself dryly.

Lady Diana was his younger sister and shared many of his physical features. The light-coloured hair, the dark-brown eyes, and the fine cheekbones that were marks of the Danvers' blood line. She was considered attractive, despite her slightly straight figure that bordered on boyish, and which was not particularly suited to the plain lines of the dress that were currently popular among ladies of her class. However, she compensated for this with her vivacious face, and there was life and a promise of fun in her dark eyes. By nature, she was far more optimistic and cheerful than her brother and, being the happy sort of woman she was (and still quite young at the tender age of twenty), her response did not disappoint him.

"I presumed you would greet the news happily," he replied to her.

"Happily? Is this the time for being happy?" The duchess interrupted. His mother was not as forthcoming or as welcoming as he had anticipated her to be. "The daughter of the Earl of Chatham is being sent to live here – to be raised in this very household?" she asked. "I do not intend to sound as though I am without heart or care, but I have yet to understand how the duty of rearing this child falls upon you. You have no wife, no woman to act as a mother to this girl. What do you plan to do about that, and why must it be *you*, who undertakes the duty of his child?"

"I have explained the circumstances," the duke said. "John has entrusted the child to me."

"You have no experience with children, and so the responsibility would fall to me and your sister, as well as to our staff. We will have to hire a governess, perhaps a nurse – if the child is not yet old enough to be attended by tutors. How old did you say she was? Someone will have to see to the procuring of these people. Have you given this endeavour any thought at all?" Her voice sounded more troubled than it had a month ago when she had found out about the love affair between her maid and a much younger stable boy.

"Am I to leave the child orphaned and alone in the world, while I decide if the cause of her abandonment and the reasons she requires my aid are valid and worthy ones?" the duke replied calmly.

"I do not care if her abandonment has been caused by a worthy or reasonable circumstance."

The duke opened his mouth to give his reply, but the duchess continued:

"Let me be clear. The reason for her predicament, while it is important, is not the primary source of my concern. Does she not have a brother, he who has inherited the title of Earl? Surely, she has family of her own, cousins perhaps, or a distant aunt, who are better suited to her care. Did they all cast her off, or are there none left alive who could care for the child?"

"I have sent a letter to the solicitor directing him to uncover the cause, as John did not disclose that matter in his letter. However, I want to be clear. Whatever the answer may be, the decision has been made. We are to offer shelter and guardianship to John's child. It is not an imposition or should not cause a moment's discord among our household or in this family. That being said–"

"Do not mistake my reason for indifference." His mother interrupted. "I am well aware that John Thornton was a dear friend of yours. I recall his father and my late husband were also the best of friends many years ago. However, my main concern is for the child's future. Has she a dowry? What will be told to her about her family? These answers must be given to us if we are to fulfil our duty to the child. She may be young now, but we must be forthcoming regarding her connections and her history if she is to one day make a good match," his mother said, ending her argument with a satisfied gleam in her eye. It was a look that Matthew knew she employed to mean that she believed she had managed to win an argument with him or his sister.

Diana ignored the serious tone of her mother as she enthused. "I care not why she has no one else, the poor little girl. How dreadful to be so young and all alone in the world. I am happy to welcome her into our home. It will be delightful to have a child to teach, and to adore. I am sure she is a pretty little thing, and musical!"

"Diana, she is not a toy, nor is she a doll," the duchess retorted. "She is a child."

"I know, Mother, but I shall endeavour to spoil her in all things, at least until the season begins, and I return to London. What a *joy* to have a child among us." Diana was undeterred.

The dowager duchess narrowed her eyes and her face relaxed. For the briefest of moments, she even seemed happy, or as happy as she could manage. Deep inside, the duchess had a warm, caring heart, but she was not prone to wild bouts of exuberance or expressions of unencumbered joy as her daughter was.

"Good," the duchess began, looking at her son. "We shall discover the details of the child's circumstances from your solicitor, of that I can be sure. However, I am pleased that you have made arrangements for the child to come to us. It seems that it has been far too long since we had a reason to be joyous in this house. The tragic loss of our dear Georgiana has hung over all of us like a grim cloud. And rightly so, she was a dear woman, whom we all adored. Nevertheless, the time for mourning her has been at an end for many years. If you cannot be persuaded to seek marriage for the sake of producing an heir, perhaps you may be persuaded by the necessity of raising a child?"

"Mother. Do not start…"

"Even with an army of servants at your disposal, you cannot serve as both Father *and* Mother to the girl – and neither can I or your sister. Your sister is unengaged, as you well know. Her future is my sole concern, as it should be yours as her brother. With our attention on Diana's prospects, the care of this child will fall on you in great part, which gives me reason to hope."

"As I said…"

"Yes, I am of the opinion that a child in this house may be what is required for you, my son. You, who have spent far too long locked away in your study, seeing to your responsibilities at the neglect of other matters. A child may be the cure for your illness. She may soften your heart that has turned to stone these many years. She may lead you to think of marriage again and of your duty concerning *your* heir."

His mother's apparent change of heart was as he suspected it would be. It was a reason to remind him of his duty, a duty he had not ignored but chose not to address. He did not have an heir, it was true, and he did not think about the issue of inheritance. How could he waste a single moment on a subject that led him to the same disagreeable place it always did, to his having to find a wife? A *wife*! He had no desire to marry. He was sure, without a doubt, that the arrival of a child, if handled in a responsible and organized manner, would not require significant changes to his household or his life except for the hiring of additional servants. Why should the presence of a child lead him to consider matrimony? He shook his head.

"How can one be so stubborn? I hope the child will not prove precocious. I recall that young John was quite a troublesome child, according to his father. Perhaps she has inherited his bad habits? What if she is wilful, or obstinate? I was told that John liked to disobey his tutors," his mother cautioned.

"Your memory is surprising, Mother," he said. "John's contempt for the rules matched my own opinion of them. We were not disobedient. We were adventurous."

"Oh, you were both stubborn *and* wilful," his mother replied. "Do not think I am excluding you. What shall be done if she is in possession of those terrible traits?"

"There is nothing to be done." The duke shrugged his shoulders and leaned back. "I will pay for her education and the expense of her nurse – should she require one – her governesses and her tutors. If she is wilful, she shall be sent to school. When she is of age, I will set a dowry, if none has been provided," he said, facing his mother. "As to the remainder of it, she is a child. What disruption can one so young and so small possibly cause among us? If there are additional concerns, I do not doubt that you, Mother, shall attend to them."

"I will help see to her. I think it will be exciting to have a child here among us," Diana jumped in before her mother could voice any further concerns. She was still excited and apparently undeterred by hiring servants and all manner of additional affairs. "It is a girl. I cannot imagine that she would be prone to misbehaving as she might if she were a boy. She will be like me, as I was when I was a child. I am certain that she will favour pretty dresses. She shall have the best dolls and toys; she will have sweets for tea. I cannot bear to wait. When will she come here to Hardwick Manor?"

"We should expect her soon." The duke's reply was vague, but that did not decrease his sister's enthusiasm.

"I shall anticipate her arrival every day!"

"Diana." The dowager duchess frowned. "You have not listened to anything I have said. The child is *not* a toy. She will be as children often are, wilful to be sure, and curious. We cannot know what education she has had, if any. If the Earl of Chatham was ill for a prolonged period, the child may have been left in the care of servants. We have no way of knowing how she was cared for, if she was taught even the most basic of manners. For all we have been told, she may be *perfectly* savage and wild."

The duke refuted that supposition straightaway. "John's daughter is not a wild animal from the forest. While we may find that she is wilful, she will undoubtedly know how to sit and eat and care for herself."

The dowager duchess raised an eyebrow in a look that suggested a contrary opinion. "How do you know that she is so well behaved?" she challenged him. "As you've explained previously, we do not know her age, or anything about her, now do we?"

"If we knew how many years she happened to have, we might already be making preparations for her inclusion into the house," Diana added.

"I do wish we knew more about the child." The duchess sighed. "Is she even walking?"

"If she is very young, perhaps she will be travelling with her nurse?"

"I cannot think that a young child would be sent in a carriage all alone." The duchess shook her head. "Perhaps she will require a cradle and nurse here as well?"

The duke rose abruptly to his feet, becoming impatient regarding his new charge. In a voice that suggested a sternness (and which could not hide his irritated tone), he addressed the women, "I have other pressing matters that require my attention. I will leave this particular one in your capable hands, Mother. Sister, any assistance that you can give will be appreciated. Children are not the domain of a duke, but of women. So it shall be in the raising of this girl child. When she is of age, I shall see that she is married to a respectable man. In the meantime, I will pay the bills associated with her care, and no more."

"That is your final word?" asked the dowager duchess. "You are leaving the whole of this endeavour in my and your sister's hands without care for my time, or your sister's own duties regarding matrimony?"

"I care, of course I do." The duke waved his hand. "Diana is a beauty in her own right and quite accomplished. She will soon find a husband, of that, I have no doubt. If I have not expressed concern, it is because I have no reason for it. However, regarding John's daughter and your time, Mother – see that what arrangements can be made are handled. Hire a governess and a nurse if you wish. The whole matter has become far more burdensome than I presumed already. I do not want to discuss the matter further."

"You are the duke – what choice do we have but to obey?" his mother answered dryly, raising her eyebrows. Matthew ignored – even though he was secretly amused by – the touch of mockery in her voice and turned to leave. They both knew his mother was not as bidd-able as she pretended at that moment.

Diana was far more joyful, and her opti-mism did not wane as she replied, "Does it matter who has the responsibility? We are to have a little girl here in our family. This is too wonderful to be believed! I will not rest until she arrives."

Despite his previous fleeting moment of joy when he considered a small child running about the house, the duke was relieved that he was no longer charged with her care or much else. His mother would see to every detail, of that he was quite sure, and his sister would as-sist her enthusiastically. All that was required from him was to pay the bills and ensure the child's basic needs were met. At the appropriate time, many years in the future, he would find the girl a husband and his promise would be fulfilled.

Glancing at the gilded mantle clock, he relaxed. There was just enough time for a brief ride on this fine afternoon. He would think no more about the girl that day. *A child in his household was not going to disrupt his schedule or much else,* he told himself as he left the drawing room.

He was completely unaware of how his life was about to change.

CHAPTER 3

$\mathcal{H}$ardwick Manor was quiet, a rarity when his mother and his sister were in residence. The two women enjoyed society. Their teas, dinners, and parties which could last for a week or more were a necessity among the duke's social set, but the duke had not enjoyed company and social obligations for many years. These days he preferred solitude to the company of others, and enjoyed riding alone, apart from the occasional hunt. He enjoyed pursuits that did not involve company except for his horse. The duke was not senti-mental about the animal, but he did think that his favourite steed, Trapper, an Irish stallion that was the pride of his stable, was probably more intelligent than most people he had met in his life.

That evening, Matthew sat in the library, a leather-bound edition of the History of the South American Continent in his hand and a brandy in a glass at his side. He enjoyed the moments of serenity that being alone afforded him.

His solicitor had yet to disclose any details of John's family – aside from sending a letter that the travel arrangements had been made. The child was supposed to have arrived at Hardwick Manor in a fortnight; however, the fortnight had come and gone, and the duke was beginning to wonder if the child was coming at all.

His mother and sister had decided to travel to London earlier in the week to meet with their milliner and dressmaker and were expected to return the following day. This was not before Diana had stretched Matthew's patience to the limit, having the servants search through the rarely opened attics for the much-loved toys and dolls of her youth. She had also toured the grounds with the gardener, discussing which tree would best serve for a swing, one that could be seen from the drawing room for supervision. Matthew had finally begged Diana to stop, after she began to wonder about having the village cabinet maker engaged to create some child-sized furniture and a doll's house. She had reluctantly agreed to await the child's arrival before ordering any further changes. For her own part, the duchess had asked the housekeeper, Mrs Claxton, to air out Diana's old room, which gave on to the front of the house with the best views.

The duke was not overly concerned about the child's late arrival, at least not yet. Perhaps an aunt had been found, or the heir to the title and the property was more generous than Matthew had assumed. *The older half-brother of the child may be a charitable man,* he decided as he let his gaze fall upon the page once more.

He settled back into the book, sipping his brandy. After the delectable dinner of roast venison, he was content to enjoy reading before retiring to bed. It was a rare pleasure these days, as it seemed to him that his mother insisted that he join her and his sister in the drawing room at every occasion. He turned the heavy page of the book, feeling the weight of the thick paper in his hand.

A footman appeared at his side, quietly as he had been trained to do. The servant, a young man, was dressed in the livery of the house Danvers. He took care not to raise his voice above a low volume, audible only to the duke, and informed the duke that a visitor had arrived at Hardwick Manor.

The duke shut the book, leaving it on the table beside his brandy as he pondered about the rather unusual time for a social call, so late in the evening and after dinner. Wait. Could it be … *her*? Without uttering a word, he stared at the footman.

The man, being a properly trained servant, had seemingly anticipated his lord's question as he added, "The Lady Isabella Thornton and company have arrived, Your Grace."

"At such a late hour?" the duke wondered. "I shall greet them in the parlour."

The footman bowed his head and left.

After several weeks of anticipating this event, Isabella had arrived at Hardwick Manor, at last. *How unfortunate that his mother and sister were not in residence to greet the child,* he thought. The two were not due to return from London until the following day, leaving him burdened with the responsibility of seeing to the child. Nevertheless, he would take it upon himself to greet the guests and determine if the girl was well. If she was fit, then his housekeeper, Mrs Claxton, could manage without him. His book and his brandy would not have to wait long, he presumed. He did not plan to tarry in the new guests' company for too long.

Dispatching the butler with a few orders, the duke told the man what must be done. "See to their bags and trunks. Send for Mrs Claxton. If she is not awake, see that she is awakened at once, I have need of her."

With his footman and butler sent about their tasks, the duke prepared himself to greet his guests. That the child was John's daughter should have been a reason for him to pause, but he was incapable of feeling any emotion other than worry. Why had the child arrived in such an untimely manner? Why could she not have arrived when his mother was in residence to attend to her?

He left the library and walked along the corridor leading to the hall.

He entered the parlour.

The silence that greeted him was not what he was expecting. He did not see anyone or hear any sound that may indicate he had a youthful visitor. He did observe that the drawing room door was ajar, however. *Would his footman have left a small child and company in the drawing room, a room filled with priceless objects such as the figurines and gilded statues that his mother adored,* he thought, worried about the child breaking something. As he approached the door, he hesitated. This was John's daughter; he did not wish to appear an old, ill-tempered man to a young girl – that would never do. Even he could see that. Willing himself to appear less imposing, he was buoyed by the fact that Mrs Claxton would arrive soon to trundle the little girl off to the nursery. The housekeeper might give her a bowl of stew or some other suitable evening meal. He smiled and willed himself to appear as benevolent and kind as he could manage before, finally, entering the room.

He was astonished by the sight before him.

Inside the drawing room, a woman stood at the opposite end by the wall of windows.

Moonlight flooded through the panes of glass, bathing her features in a soft glow. Her pale skin was illuminated by the soft light, and her brown hair glistened, as all around the moonlight danced and played, making her appear like an angel, despite her being dressed in the dark garb of mourning. She must not have heard him approach because she did not turn to face him. She remained with her face lifted towards the light.

He stood, motionless, appreciating the statuesque figure of the beauty who slowly opened her eyes, as if she were enraptured by the view of the full moon on the lawn that lay just beyond the window. As he observed her, watching for any indication that she was a ghostly form or the result of his imagination, he dared not speak. He was awestruck by her, as he would be of a magnificent view of a painting.

Matthew was accustomed to being in complete control of all that he felt and all that he surveyed. Yet, at this moment, as he stared at the beautiful woman, who stood unaware of his observation, he was lost for words. However, it was but only for a moment. He quickly quelled the emotion he felt welling within. He dismissed his own reaction to her as astonishment, at having a visitor so late in the evening and nothing more. He was a duke, for heaven's sake, he was not a boy besot by beauty. He was not in the habit of feeling awed for *any* reason. He was not one to stand in stupefaction gazing at the beauty in front of him. It was time to address her.

"My footman informed me that I have a visitor. Whom am I addressing?" he asked formally. "Have you arrived with the child?"

She turned to face him – her deep-blue eyes were as pleasant as the graceful features of her oval face. *Who was this young woman – the child's nurse or her governess, perhaps?* He wondered, even though her wardrobe did not announce her to be either of those.

She lowered her head and curtsied. "It is a pleasure to make your acquaintance, Your

Grace. I am Isabella Thornton, the daughter of the Earl of Chatham."

He stood silent, trying to make sense of her words.

"I have travelled with my maid. I believe she is seeing to the matter of my trunks," she continued, her voice as delightful as music played gently on a harp.

"*You* are Isabella Thornton?" he asked as he tried to reconcile the woman who was standing in front of him with the image of a young child.

"I am known as Lady Isabella, Sir." She smiled. "I was told that you were expecting me."

"How old are you?"

"I have one and twenty years, Sir," she replied, seemingly surprised by his presumptuous question.

His first impulse was to express his astonishment that she – and not a diminutive eight-year-old – was standing in his drawing room, but he regained full control of his emotions and his words. While her beauty and her natural vivaciousness were attractive traits, they were not enough to convince him that his responsibility to her was anything other than that – a duty to be performed like all the other duties that filled his schedule.

"I will not bore you with the details, but we did not anticipate your arrival at such a late hour," he replied with hardly any trace of warmth. "If you would like to avail yourself of tea and refreshment, the housekeeper will see that your trunks are taken up to your room in the meantime. You mentioned a maid – will she be remaining in your employ?"

The smile that had made Lady Isabella's features even more pleasant mere moments ago, faded, and her face became set in a determined manner. "My maid will be remaining in my employ. She is indispensable to me."

"Very well," the duke replied as he continued to study her.

Her mother, he decided, must have been a beauty. The woman he saw standing before him seemed to bear no trace of his dear friend John's features – except possibly for the colour of her hair. It was a shade of dark brown that complemented her rosy cheeks and her fine porcelain complexion.

"Welcome to Hardwick Manor, Lady Isabella," he said.

The duke recalled that he intended to fulfil his promise to John, but still he allowed a faint smile to pass his face. It came from his silent relief that his friend's daughter was not a child. It was true, somewhere deep inside – very deep, in fact – the laughter and innocence of a child had been anticipated with interest. He could not deny it. But he was not so optimistic that he could be persuaded that children required anything less than an army of servants and attention, compared to a grown woman. With the beauty and natural grace that Isabella Thornton possessed, the only thing left for him to accomplish would be to find a husband for her. He was sure his mother would assume that task with both pleasure *and* dedication.

The duke felt grateful, for that would be a matter of little consequence – and bother – to him. So grateful, in fact, that he allowed himself a few more sentences of conversation with her. Her countenance was pleasing. The young woman did not offer apologies or recede into platitudes in the silence that soon fell between them. Instead, she stood as though she was not his subordinate, but rather his equal – as a woman who belonged in the drawing room of one of the finest country houses in all of England.

He nearly smiled again to think that she might be as wilful and disobedient as her father. The thought brought Matthew back to an unaddressed question that neither the young woman nor his solicitor had answered in the weeks preceding her arrival. Since Isabella Thornton was a woman and not a child, why did she require the care and guardianship that his rank and title afforded? Was she not related to the gentleman who had inherited the title of the Earl of Chatham, and so by all accounts should she not be legally provided for by him?

The duke glanced at the clock on the mantle, with its gilded case and gold-trimmed hands. The hour was late. Lady Isabella must surely be fatigued from her journey. It was not the time to discuss such matters. Getting answers would need to wait a little longer.

CHAPTER 4

The Lady Isabella Thornton, recent arrival at Hardwick Manor, awoke when the first rays of the sun touched the house. She opened her eyes and yawned as the room was bathed in the golden light that accompanied dawn at that time of year. She was astonished that she had slept very well. She had no reason to be awake at this ridiculous hour, but she felt rested despite the early morning. The carriage ride across roads that were rutted and muddy from the recent summer storms meant that she had been unable to find the trip as restful as she might have if the way had been more pleasant. Perhaps, she mused, it was because of the difficult journey, that she had found sleep so easily, after finally making her way up the grand staircase to her room.

Isabella lifted her head from her pillow and took stock of her surroundings, something she had failed to do a few hours earlier. When she had first walked into the room, the immense space had been dark except for a few candles in sconces and a small fire that burned in the hearth. Now, in the morning light, she observed that the room she had been given was panelled in dark wood. It was the same wood as the carved posters of her bed, which was immense and heavily built.

The windows were quite old. She could tell from the circles in the glass, a mark of the older glass maker's art. Her father, an educated and eccentric man, whom she had adored, had taken great delight in drawing her attention to points of architecture, such as this odd trivial detail. She had eagerly soaked up these particulars when she was a child, as he imparted his knowledge while they visited cathedrals or important historic buildings during their travels. He was an unusual person, travelling to the colonies and ports near and far, even permitting her to accompany him on his trips, especially after the tragedy of her mother's death. She remembered those days with fondness. How she missed those journeys! The smell of the salt air, the adventures, the foreign lands…

Isabella closed her eyes. She sighed, knowing that was all behind her. The days of travelling in the company of her father – those days were over.

The alteration in her circumstances had come so harshly and abruptly after her father's death. She wished to forget all about the sorrow she had known, even if it meant dismissing the wonderful memories she had of her adventures in her father's company – adventures she might one day revisit, but not yet. The pain of losing him was still fresh, and the loneliness that gripped her was far too powerful to permit her a few moments of comfort, such as dwelling on fond remembrances of the past.

She rubbed her eyes and tried not to think of her father or the tragic circumstances that led her to Hardwick Manor. She was alone in the world, all alone. If she dwelt upon that fact, she knew she could become despondent. When the duke had asked her if she would be keeping her maid, she had responded without a moment's hesitation. She had not added that she would retain Mary, even if it cost her *every* penny she had. However, her own funds were rather meagre and scarcely enough to afford to employ Mary, much less keep her in the manner to which she was accustomed, as the daughter of an Earl. Unknown to the duke, or indeed anyone else, Mary was much more than a maid to Isabella. Not only was she a trusted servant, but she was also a confidante who genuinely cared about her. Mary was the last link to the life she once led when she was a beloved daughter.

Leaving behind the unfamiliar bed, she walked to the window, where she was pleased to find a window seat with a beautiful view. She knelt upon the cushions and looked out. The view was breath-taking. Beyond the immense gardens, she saw a lawn that stretched for miles. Although she could not see them from her current vantage point, she was sure there were pools and fountains. She hoped she could see the fountains during a stroll that morning as she became acquainted with her new home or, at least, her home until she married.

"Marriage." She sighed, her one prospect. She supposed she could become a governess, or a ladies' companion. Those positions did not appeal to her, but they did afford a mode of independence, if not respect. She was well read and smart. She enjoyed taking part in conversations that often covered topics not normally considered suitable for the ladies' drawing room. Her father had enjoyed discussing the topics of the day with her, and from an early age, she had sought additional amusement other than what sewing and playing the piano afforded. She was aware that her adoration of books and her love of knowledge made her different from the few women who she knew well. Given her father's long illness, she had not entered society properly, nor had she enjoyed a season in London, as was the custom for girls of her age and class. However, at the age of one and twenty, it was not yet too late to find a husband, should she wish to do so.

Still, without much in the way of a dowry or a title of her own, she was not sure how well she would fare in the London marriage market. She detested using that phrase "marriage market" – it reminded her of a cow market – but the description was an apt one. It seemed to express the singular occupation of every unmarried woman over the age of eighteen, and that was to find and capture a husband. She had even heard the term clearly used to explain the mercenary and cold nature of the pursuit of matrimony. It enticed hundreds of well-to-do young women to London, and Bath, and nearly every other large metropolis that boasted any sort of a social season.

Of course, she knew (as did every other woman born to status) that any place that was not London did not offer the same prospects as the capital for finding a truly suitable husband. Isabella could claim a close connection to the Earl of Chatham, but she had no real measurable wealth or large tracts of property.

Wrapping her arms around herself, she found the thin material of her nightgown did little to keep her warm. Yet, she did not want to leave the window with its magnificent view, not while she considered her future. If she could come to terms with her reduced circumstances, perhaps she might advertise for a position. There was nothing keeping her from absenting herself from the pursuit of a husband

and all that it entailed. *Reduced circumstances!* It was ironic to think that she, the daughter of nobility and the ward of a duke, considered herself to be in reduced circumstances. However, it was the truth, regardless of how she wished it were otherwise. At the moment, she was utterly dependent on the kindness and generosity of the Duke of Devonshire.

She wondered how differently her meeting with the duke might have gone, had she been introduced to him on different terms. The conversation with him had been stilted, polite, and thoroughly predictable. He had enquired after her journey, her maid's salary (which he had generously offered to pay, while Isabella remained his ward), and he had asked if she wished for anything to be brought to her room, aside from the tea that they had taken in the drawing room. Then, as quickly as could be managed, he had graciously retired, leaving her in the capable hands of the housekeeper (who seemed as shocked to see her as the duke had been when she had first spoken to him).

. . .

A QUIET KNOCK SOUNDED, and then the door of her bedroom opened slowly with a creaking sound that was barely audible. She was unsure who could be entering her room so early in the morning and steeled herself for whoever might be intruding upon her. She was relieved to see a familiar face.

"Mary! You gave me a fright!" Isabella said to the woman who came bustling into the room, a sombre-coloured dress draped over her arm.

The maid was older than Isabella, perhaps by three decades or even more. Her brown-silver hair was pulled back under a plain white cap. Her dark dress fitted snuggly over her tall, rounded frame. She was not a beauty, but her smile was pleasing, and her features were not without merit.

Mary exclaimed at the sight of her mistress, "Miss! I did not expect to find you out of your bed at such a time. I was on my way downstairs to press this afternoon frock when the scullery maid told me she thought you were awake. The poor dear girl, she was scared she had woken you."

"That dear girl, she most certainly did not waken me. I rested very well and was awake at a surprisingly early hour," Isabella admitted.

"I wish that I could say the same, for I did not rest. I should have, after *that* carriage ride. Never have I had a bumpier ride... except for crossing the channel from Dublin town. My bottom is hurting just thinking about it." She winked at Isabella, who could not help but laugh at her maid's frank comment.

"Mary, perhaps you shall do better this evening once you are settled. Not that I shall ever quite feel settled here. Did you see how the duke looked at me last night? I believe he was expecting a far younger person! He asked my age, can you believe, as directly as if he were asking if I would like tea? As if that were not a surprise enough to me, he slipped away as quickly as he could and left the housekeeper to see to me."

"I can scarcely believe it, *Miss.*"

"Have you not seen him yet?"

"I have neither seen the master of the house myself, nor have I heard anything about him from the servant's hall. Not that I mean any disrespect to His Grace, but his servants were all in bed, except for the housekeeper, and she was concerning herself with you."

Sighing, Isabella replied, "I suppose it is unimportant whether I was presumed to be a child or myself. What concerns me at present is tea – I should like a cup."

"As I mentioned, I was on my way to press this frock for the afternoon, but I *have* heard from the maids that unmarried ladies take their breakfast and tea downstairs. I replied that that was all well and good, but if you asked me for a spot of tea in your room, with some bread and jam, then I could not deny you. Should I see to a pot of tea? It would ward off any chill you might have caught from the night air last evening."

"I will dress and go downstairs, for when the breakfast is served. I do not want to give the wrong impression to His Grace. Not on any account. However, if you arrange a cup of tea while I am getting ready, I would be delighted."

Mary beamed at Isabella and replied cheerfully, "A cup of good strong tea will be just the thing. I shall see that the cook knows what she is about. We will not have any weak tea today."

Isabella smiled at the older woman, feeling a surge of gratitude towards her. Mary was worth every penny of her salary. What would Isabella do without her, especially now that she was alone in the world, without her father or mother, and only her half-brother ... although, well, that was another matter altogether.

Hardwick Manor was her new home, she told herself. How could she ever manage to call it home when her own was so far away? She gazed at the door, fervently wishing for Mary to return with that cup of tea. She was in desperate need of its warm comfort, to fortify herself for the day ahead in these unknown surroundings. She needed comfort before she saw His Grace once more. She was certain the man considered her to be little more than a bother.

CHAPTER 5

*B*reakfast was uneventful. The duke appeared and greeted her in a customary polite fashion, asking her the expected questions. Had she rested well? Did she enjoy the view of the gardens which were visible from that part of the house? A view he said was one of the best at Hardwick Manor. She answered his questions, taking care not to be too bold with her manners – she did not wish to incur any censure or to give him a bad impression of her. In addition to her genuine desire to please him and to be accepted into the family, she realised that she was dependent on him for her livelihood, and so she was polite, rather than relaxed. Polite conversation and demure manners came naturally to her, despite being a young woman who was known throughout her former household as one who possessed an independent nature.

She hoped that after breakfast, she would be free to roam the house and grounds. She wished to learn all about Hardwick Manor, and to gain a sense of the place, so that she could understand its ways and accustom herself to her new life.

The duke followed the protocols of their class to the letter, it seemed. Straight after breakfast, he escorted her on a brief but dispassionate tour of the house and the close gardens. When she asked him polite questions about the history of the residence, of his family or his title, the duke took care to look at her only briefly. He was just as she had come to expect upper-class gentlemen of rank to be: cold, polite, and exceedingly disinterested in anything she (or any other woman, for that matter) had to say. It was not that he acted badly towards her, but she did not feel any warmth in his words. The man – who may have been handsome if he had only chosen to smile – performed his social obligations towards her in the same perfunctory manner as if he were overseeing accounts or reviewing his business matters. Isabella nearly giggled at that thought. Perhaps he *enjoyed* managing his estate far more than he enjoyed her company. At least, it appeared to be so, as he discussed the history of the garden architecture and the follies, all the while avoiding her direct regard.

The one subject, however, about which the Duke did speak with enthusiasm was Trapper. When they passed through the stables, the subject of the horse and his champion pedigree was shared in a much more animated tone, and in such a way as to suggest that there may be more to the duke than his title and his duty. According to the Duke of Devonshire, Trapper was a magnificent animal of racing stock, and also possessed a strong and admirable character.

The day was beautiful, the weather had warmed considerably, and Isabella longed to ride the sleek horse. The duke did not make mention of her accompanying him on a ride but did ask whether she had brought along her riding habit. Perhaps it was her black mourning dress that caused him to abstain from inquiries regarding her interests, accomplishments, or hobbies? In fact, she found it odd that he had not asked her about herself at all and had barely responded to any of her questions about the architecture or the landscaping. Instead, he continued his tour, noting important facts without much care for whether she was amused, entertained, or bored.

Who was this man, she wondered as they returned to the house from the stables? She did not find him to be the adventurous sort of man her father had described him to be. He was remarkably different from the gentlemen she expected to find waiting for her upon her arrival.

Her father had often spoken of the duke as though he was a man who enjoyed a great range of interests and was rather gregarious and charming. She found the man standing before her to be neither gregarious nor charming. *If* he was in possession of any interests, other than riding, he hid them perfectly well. It was pitiable that he should be so tedious and formal, when she had to admit to herself that she found him slightly dashing – no matter how distant his disposition.

"If you will accompany me to the drawing room, my mother and sister are due to return at any hour. They have been anxiously awaiting your arrival."

"Do you wish me to wait for them in the drawing room?" she asked and offered a warm smile. "Will you be accompanying me?"

He looked at her in a rather odd way and gave a nod. "It is my duty to attend to you as my guest, until they arrive."

Perhaps it was the tedium of the tour, but she broke with decorum as she candidly remarked, "If you have other duties which require your attention, Sir, I shall not blame you for seeing to them instead. If I am given a book and a cup of tea, I will do very well. I am perfectly accustomed to attending to my own amusement."

She wanted to add that, in fact, she *preferred* her own company to his dour expression and lack of interest in, or, anything about her, but she remained silent. He was her father's dear friend, and yet he had not made any inquiries about the circumstances of her father's death. Isabella was willing to accept that such questions may have been unseemly, but the duke did not appear to have any interest in her father or her life.

"My other duties are not pressing," he answered her question.

For a short moment, Isabella was surprised by his answer, believing he would agree to her proposal. As he had not, she resigned herself to his company until his mother and his sister arrived. Side-by-side, they walked to the drawing room, and Isabella sat by the fireside. As the clock ticked loudly on the mantle, she decided to address him with slightly less tact than may have been proper.

"My father often spoke to me of this house. He was very fond of it. I had hopes that you might share some of your memories of your friendship with him, or stories of your adventures. My father often said you and he were fond of trouble."

The duke studied her with a look whose nature she could not discern. "Those days are long past."

"Oh," she answered quickly, "forgive me. I did not mean to intrude. I feel his loss keenly, and it has been painful for me to relive the memories I possess of him. I was hoping that you might share tales of his childhood, which might bring some comfort. If I have intruded upon your feelings regarding my father or your own sorrow, I offer my sincerest apology."

The clock on the mantle continued to mark the minutes and hours, the sound of it ticking away the time as she awaited his response be it good or ill. Finally, he answered: "There is no need for an apology. It is natural that you should be curious about the man who was your father."

Following that succinct statement, he fell quiet again, and so did she as she realised that she would learn nothing more from the duke, that was, nothing he did not wish to disclose. Without conversation or a book to distract her, she studied the furnishings and decorations of the room. The paintings on the walls were superb, and the figurines were undoubtedly priceless, but none seemed to be subjects of note that the duke might care to discuss. She made an effort to find a topic on which he might converse at length, until the arrival of his family. Isabella anticipated the event with some nervousness, as she fervently prayed that his mother and his sister would be far more agreeable than the man now seated across from her.

It was pitiable she should find him so unapproachable. From what little she knew of him, from her brief acquaintance, she had already formed an opinion of him as a man who possessed an imposing presence. His features were chiselled and handsome, his eyes were piercing and dark, and could be described as riveting. He was just the sort of man she envisioned when she was reading novels, as a hero or a villain depending upon the story.

Most interesting, and contrary to her experience of her father's acquaintances, he seemed completely and utterly impervious to her charms or her beauty. This was not vanity – she knew that other men found her engaging and unusual in her interests and conversation. She had also been complimented on her looks often enough to know that men found her appearance pleasant. The duke, however, seemed blind to her looks and unconcerned about engaging her in any type of conversation.

"The tour of your house and grounds was enriching," she replied, searching for any word to say other than what she thought, which was *perfunctory.* "Are there any other remarkable details of the architecture or the planning of the grounds which you may not have mentioned?"

"Do you find your room satisfactory?" he asked.

"Yes, thank you," she answered, once again coming to an impasse. He did not appear to be interested in conversing other than to exchange a few uncomfortable sentences.

Peering at him, she wondered what was to be done to broach his reticence towards her. She did not have long to ponder that question. When she turned towards the doorway, she noticed that the silence that had settled awkwardly between them was being interrupted by the sound of women's voices, coming from outside the drawing room.

"She is here, at last!"

Isabella heard the unmistakable tone of voice that indicated excitement, and this exclamation was followed by a voice that could only be the duke's mother.

"Diana. Do be mindful of your position. You are a lady – I do wish you would act as one."

The anticipated arrival of the dowager duchess and her daughter was not entirely as Isabella had expected. The duchess was not as stern as she assumed a woman in possession of such an esteemed title might be (especially after she had met the duke), and her daughter was not at all the sort of woman who was re-strained by decorum, as one might expect. In appearance, the young woman's features and hair were the same as the duke's, with one no-ticeable difference. His sister, whom Isabella judged to be about her age, or at least very near to it, was smiling with joy, from cheek to cheek.

The duke made the necessary introductions, in his straightforward manner, as the younger woman studied Isabella with unabashed glee, and the older woman wore her surprise in a less conspicuous manner.

Without the slightest concern for reserve, Diana exclaimed, "Mother, look! Forgive us for staring, but we were expecting a child, not a woman. How extraordinary!"

Whereas the dowager duchess appeared to be astonished, she was not as forthcoming in her expression of it. It seemed to Isabella that nothing in the world could possibly give her cause for any outward sign of surprise. Her perfect composure was a mark of the upper classes, who attempted to maintain proper decorum at all times. Isabella began to see similarities between the duchess and her son.

"I trust you are settling into your room, and all is well?" the duchess asked Isabella.

"Yes, thank you," Isabella replied. "I am well pleased."

"Diana, ring for tea, and we shall all become acquainted with Lady Isabella after we have changed from our travelling clothes," the duchess said to her daughter.

"Please do excuse us, Lady Isabella." Diana managed to add the courtesy before a look from her mother hastened her exit.

Watching the two women leave the room,

Isabella did not relish spending time alone with the duke again, and she anticipated the same silence between them. Fortunately, she did not have long to wait in his cool and quiet company. In her opinion, he was undoubtedly performing his duty in remaining with her until his mother and sister could return.

They managed this rather quickly, given that they both returned attired in quite sumptuous frocks. Diana's dress had slightly more of a skirt than was fashionable, and the bodice was intricately embroidered. Isabella astutely surmised that these alterations had been made to lend a more feminine shape to the young slender woman. This observation told her much about how Lady Diana saw herself, and Isabella warmed towards the young woman who would be, to all intents and purposes, her new sister.

The duchess and her daughter welcomed Isabella into their home, with a mixture of restrained warmth from the duchess and near exuberance from Lady Diana. Diana, who had greeted Isabella so joyously, was now enthusiastically discussing all manner of subjects that ladies from well-bred families would find amusing, such as the upcoming season and fashion. Isabella found the welcome she had received from the women of the Danvers family far surpassed the coldness of the duke's reception.

Without much response from his sister or mother and barely a glance from Isabella, the duke made his excuses and slipped from the drawing room. Isabella watched him from the corner of her eye, curious but unaware that what she presumed was arrogance and distance were much more than that. Nevertheless, she did not want to think about him anymore that day, especially now that she had been reminded, once again, of what it was like to be among friendly and kind people. How comforting it felt to discuss all matters of subjects with a woman such as the Duchess of Devonshire and her daughter, who promised to be as good a sister as Isabella might have wished.

The duke's lack of a warm welcome was nearly forgotten, as Isabella smiled truly for the first time in weeks. Speaking of subjects that were not serious in nature, such as dresses, bonnets, and novels, helped to banish the sadness that haunted her, however, her father's loss could not be so easily forgotten in a few hours' conversation and companionship.

"I must apologize that I had quite forgotten that you were in mourning. Dear me," the duke's sister said. "How dreadful for you. Here I am discussing the styles of gowns, and satins and silks, and you have been through so much. I am so thoughtless at times – it is one of my great faults."

Isabella smiled at Lady Diana kindly. "Do not think for a moment that I am offended by the gaiety of the discussion or the cheer that you have brought to me. The conversation has done me an undeniable good."

The duchess's butler poured another cup of tea. "Have you been in mourning for long?" the duchess asked carefully. "I apologise for asking such a tactless question, but I was not given any information about the situation in which you now find yourself, except that your father has recently passed away."

"Will you be in mourning throughout the season?" Lady Diana added. "I know that is an equally terrible question, but we cannot be in society together if you are, it would be too horrid an imposition on you."

The younger woman's question was met with a stern expression from her mother as Isabella answered, "I have not been in mourning for very long. It is but two more months and no longer. However, I believe I will no longer be in this sad state when the season begins in the New Year."

"Then, you shall accompany us to London," Lady Diana responded. "If you feel so inclined, we may give a few modest dinners before that, so that you may become acquainted with the society here at Hardwick Manor, and that they understand that you are now a member of our house. It may not be entirely proper, but you could be quietly introduced to the local gentry."

Isabella was truly appreciative of the young woman's wish to cheer her and to welcome her to the family. "Thank you. That would be a welcome diversion."

After a pause, she continued in a slightly lower tone, "My father was a singular man, you must understand. He would not have wished for me to be saddened or despairing for an exceedingly long period of time. He said as much to me after my mother died, and so I presume he must have meant it for himself, as well. That may sound terribly cavalier, but I assure you that my mother and father were both the best of people, and they cared for me a great deal. I have felt their loss more keenly than anyone can know, and yet it is that same love they offered me that helps me to bear their loss. I know that their love continues, and I like to think that it is possible they are still looking after me through that sentiment. I have come to understand that there is a great deal of comfort to be found in joyous memories of past times."

She noticed the gleam of unshed tears in Diana's sympathetic eyes and hastened to bring the conversation back to a happier keel. "It is with gratitude that I welcome any introduction that you may make on my behalf, until such time as I am no longer in mourning, when I may attend balls and larger gatherings."

"Your words are very well put, my dear," the duchess replied, leaning slightly towards Isabella to indicate her own agreement and sympathy. Privately, she wondered how it was that this young woman had already seized grief's lesson so well, in a few short months, when her own son had not done so in years.

"I am glad to hear you say so," Diana added. "We shall take care not to overburden you during this time, but the weather is simply too beautiful to be ignored. Would you consider a picnic to cheer you?" Lady Diana asked, her eyes gleaming at the prospect.

"Thank you. I would like that very much,"

Isabella replied. She already felt the beginning of a bond – a camaraderie – between herself and Lady Diana. When she thought of her own half-brother, she quickly tried to rid her mind of him and her speculation of what may have become of him since he had become the next Earl.

"Splendid! Isn't it splendid, Mother?" Lady Diana was unapologetically happy about the picnic, which brightened Isabella's mood.

If she thought of nothing more than the picnic, she was almost able to forget the duke's coldness and the reason she had come to Hardwick Manor in the first place.

CHAPTER 6

"It is hardly customary to make introductions to a person who is in mourning, however, in this circumstance it cannot be helped," the duchess explained to the older couple.

Isabella did not think the duchess was aware that she had overheard her conversation. From the vantage point of where she was standing, on the banks of the river that ran through the village green of Beyton Dale, she did not think anyone had observed her at all. To Isabella's delight, Beyton Dale was as idyllic a village as any she could have imagined. From its stone church, to the Tudor buildings on high street, to the green that bordered the river, she found the whole of the hamlet to be charming.

The weather was beautiful for the time of year, and the setting could not have been more tranquil. Trees were filled with foliage that shaded visitors to the village that day. Isabella had found a few minutes of peace in a secluded spot by the river. She inhaled the sweet scent of the flowers and was glad that she had found so aromatic a place to sit unobserved. Sunlight filtered through the branches, creating a lovely shimmering effect on the water of the river. The large bushes around her were in full bloom. Although she was not particularly in need of solitude, she sometimes craved it, especially these days, as her thoughts were rather confused. The dark-green leaves concealed Isabella as she watched the water drift by. This was the same river she recalled that her father had mentioned in tales from his youth.

"The poor lamb, how tragic to be so young,

and to have seen so much loss," the kindly older woman said in response to the Duchess of Devonshire. Isabella silently chided herself for listening to a conversation which was surely meant to be private. Yet, her curiosity was overwhelming. It had been nearly a fortnight since she arrived at Hardwick Manor, and she marvelled as to the true and honest nature of the people who now cared for her as though she was a cousin or a dear friend.

Isabella recognised the voice of the duchess in response. "Of course, we will have to order her a new wardrobe, once she comes out of mourning. The clothes she brought with her to Hardwick Manor are all in mourning colours. Her others are dyed in equally sombre hues. In London, she will require the very best gowns in order to secure a husband. I have spoken to my son about it and, of course, he agrees to my suggestion."

"Naturally, she should have some nice things of her own, after losing her parents and her home." The answer given by the kindly older woman cheered Isabella. "Has she no other relatives? Is she truly all alone in this world?"

"She is survived by no other close family, except for an older half-brother by the earl's first wife. I do not know much about him," the dowager duchess answered. "I have heard that he has inherited the property and the title."

"Oh. Is that so?"

"Strangely enough, I was told that he was last seen at the Port of Hastings, but I have never been one for gossip."

Isabella, who had been considering stealthily sneaking away before anyone noticed she was listening to the conversation, nearly stopped breathing. *What was known of her half-brother,* she wondered? She heard the cheerful voice of Lady Diana joining in the conversation. She wanted to hear more about him, but she had to admit that Lady Diana's inclusion into the conversation would be the perfect time for her to make an appearance, as well. She reasoned that her arrival might go unnoticed, and by the same token, so would her concealment.

"Mr and Mrs Price, how lovely to see you." She overheard Lady Diana say to the older couple, who returned the greeting.

Isabella brushed the grass from the inky-black cloth of her afternoon dress. On days such as today she did not mind it so much, although it did seem as if the cloth was awfully warm under the summer sun. Her clothes had been the cause of many a glance, without introductions to follow, from the people on the green who were enjoying the day. She was actually surprised that the elderly couple had come to greet the duchess, but she presumed it was due to their long-time acquaintance. It was an assumption she made from the easy manner in which she heard the couple speaking to the duchess and Lady Diana – both women who were far superior to them in rank.

As unobtrusively as she could, she walked the long way around from the riverbank and emerged onto the path. Immediately, she found herself being greeted by Lady Diana who left the company of her mother and the Prices to approach Isabella gleefully. That was, as gleefully as one might when speaking to someone who was dressed in the sombre colours of mourning in public.

"Lady Isabella, I have been searching *everywhere* on the green for you. Wherever did you manage to hide?" Lady Diana gave her a big smile. When Isabella seemed to stumble for an answer, she continued, "Oh, that is not important, not when I have much to tell you." She lowered her tone of voice. "It seems that despite your unfortunate state, you have managed to catch the eye of several young gentlemen. They cannot come to greet you, however, as they have not been formally introduced, and you are in mourning."

Isabella gave her a surprised nod. "I have?"

"You will be a success in London." The duchess's voice sounded behind them, and the two young women turned to face her.

"Mr Price, Mrs Price. May I introduce the

Lady Isabella Thornton? She is our guest and ward at Hardwick Manor," the duchess said in a pleasant tone of voice.

"It is delightful to make your acquaintance," Mrs Price remarked, and Mr Price bowed. "Please accept our deepest condolences on your loss. I met your father several times and found him to be a true and worthy gentleman," Mr Price added in a soft tone.

"My, you are a pretty young lady," Mrs Price said and smiled.

Isabella smiled warmly at the pair.

"I can hardly bear to wait." Lady Diana's enthusiasm continued into her words as she returned to her subject. "If you are already admired in this village dressed as you are, then I am certain you will be the belle of the town when we arrive in London for the season. My clothes will be finished in a month, apart from the fitting, and then we shall see to ordering your wardrobe. Mother has said so! Is that not good news?"

Isabella's head was nearly spinning with Diana's exuberant predictions. Her light-hearted and relatively untempered demeanour led Isabella to guess that the young woman had never actually spent a season in London. *A season amongst the social elite might temper her nature and her outbursts*, she remembered the duchess's words, but Isabella found herself hoping that nothing would change the sunny outlook of the young woman she had grown so fond of.

Remembering to sound surprised about her wardrobe, which she knew she ought not have overheard, Isabella remarked, "I appreciate the charming gesture, but it is one I neither deserve … nor would ever ask to receive. It would not be proper for His Grace to purchase my wardrobe. Are my own clothes not suitable?"

"Suitable? My dear, what could you hope to find in your wardrobe when all of your clothes are in similar shades, appropriate to your grief?" the duchess remarked in a firm but not unkind way. "You are in urgent need of new dresses, child."

Strangely enough, it was Mr Price who gave the agreeing nod. Isabella did not know if he really agreed with the duchess or if he just wanted to be a part of the conversation, which was beginning to stray from the boundaries of any man's interest. Perhaps he had agreed simply to move the topic along. She smiled to herself.

Diana pouted a little, but it was in jest. "Why would you not permit my brother to see to it that you are provided with lovely new dresses? I do not wish to seem indiscrete and common, but he is perfectly capable of paying for a few gowns."

"Diana, it is not polite to speak of these things," the duchess said and earned an apologetic frown from her daughter and an amused glance from Mr Price.

However, Lady Diana had spoken the truth. Her dark eyes were narrowed in concentration as she considered the London season to be of the utmost importance. The perfect selection of dresses was critical to any young woman who wished to find a husband. Isabella knew that it was Diana's sincere wish to help her, and her offers of advice were not painful to bear, given as they were with her indefatigable optimism.

"In London, new dresses are purchased for no other purpose but to adorn and display a woman's figure, wealth, and taste," the duchess remarked, and Mrs Price nodded eagerly.

To show that she was not in any way perturbed by the duchess and her friends' wishes to be helpful, Isabella attempted to turn the conversation in a different direction. "I have heard the same, but frankly, I would consider it a waste to have a dress that I could wear but one or two times, and then only in London. Surely one such dress is enough, with perhaps several others that might be worn on many occasions."

The duchess and Mrs Price nodded their agreement, and Mrs Price began a story of a dress she had loved and had had remade to wear after the season had ended. Mr Price stood beside her, nodding, and saying nothing

– the ladies were now midstream in a river where he could neither navigate nor change the flow.

Isabella turned back towards Diana and leaned in. "Tell me about those gentlemen, whom you observed stealing glances?" she asked the young woman.

"I long to," Diana answered rather melodramatically, "but without boring our friends here." She took a hold of Isabella's arm and pulled her to the side a little. Isabella allowed Diana to lead her away a few steps before she glanced back – almost too obviously – to make sure they were out of ear shot of the duchess and her friends. They were far from anyone who might be listening.

Lady Diana turned her beaming face back to Isabella. "There were ever so many!"

"Are you certain of this?"

"Not all of them could be introduced, even if you were not in mourning, as I said. I saw merchants and the son of the local doctor – but there was a baronet."

"A baronet?"

"Yes. A most amiable nobleman from just outside Beyton Dale," her excitement dropped then, as she added, "however, even if you were not dressed so drearily, and if we *had already been* introduced into society, they would still not *dare* to approach either you or me here in the village. But, I am certain that they wished they might, especially the baronet. Surely you recall seeing him? He was handsome, was he not? I found him to be handsome, although you or others may not find him so." She was obviously warming to her subject, and her eyes wandered off in blissful thought. "I have to admit, while he may not be the most handsome man by the usual standards, he looks charismatic, and he has a muscular build. He is a colonel in the guards and recently returned from the war, where I hear he distinguished himself most valiantly. He has a striking figure, and he is fashionable. He was staring at you in a way that I found most romantic."

"Why should they hesitate to speak to us?"

asked Isabella, returning to Diana's first comment.

"My brother, my dear Isabella." Lady Diana did not hesitate in her response.

She looked toward the duchess and then glanced around, presumably to watch out for the duke himself and to make sure he could not hear, but there was no sign of him.

"He is the reason for their reticence, I fear. He can be rather *imposing*."

"Is it his rank which makes him seem so …" Isabella searched for the right word, although "terrifying" would not have been appropriate, "… stringent in his opinions? I presume he enjoys the highest rank in this county."

"I suppose you must be right." Diana leaned in closer to Isabella and said quietly, "His rank and title are rather intimidating, but then, so is he. I probably should not be saying this because he is my own dear brother, but if you watch him, you will soon notice that he rarely smiles, or engages in pleasantries. I must confess that I am *astonished* that he came to the picnic in our company today. Astonished!" She repeated the word, and Isabella assumed it was to make sure that she grasped the unusualness of the situation. "Were he not here today, I am certain we may have been delighted to have made the acquaintance of at least one gentleman who was daring enough to introduce himself!"

"Where *is* His Grace? I do not see him, much less observe him engaged in fending away any forward suitors," Isabella said, smiling as she glanced at the small group comprised of the dowager duchess and the Prices.

"He must have taken his leave to speak to the vicar, but there he is now, approaching us." Lady Diana gestured towards the Duke of Devonshire who was walking towards them from the direction of the nearby church and vicarage, which shared a low-stone wall with the village green.

Without being aware of her reasoning, or indeed, her actions, Isabella's fingers touched her hair, which was still safely tucked into her bonnet. Why was she worried about her appearance when she was dressed in black? She knew that to anyone who observed her, she must appear to be that of a sad raven, compared to Lady Diana who was dressed in yards of pretty white material embroidered with a hundred delicate rosebuds. Dropping her hand to her side, she curtsied as she did when greeting the duke, and then gave him a direct gaze.

Even though he chose to acknowledge her with the most rudimentary of exchanges, no one had said nor implied the dreary spectre Isabella had imagined herself to be, and certainly not the duchess, Lady Diana, or the duke himself. Yet, Isabella felt it hovering unsaid every time he spoke to her.

It seemed to her that she was treated far better by his sister, who by all rights had no reason to be friendly towards her. In addition, the duchess could have resented her as an interloper. Instead, these two women had shown her compassion and kindness. The man who should have been her champion, who agreed to care for her (for a reason she still could not understand), seemed to consider her to be little more than a burden – a debt owed to a creditor.

"I have been looking for you, dear brother." Diana's voice was bright and innocent as ever.

The duke greeted his sister with a smile and gave Isabella a quick bow.

"Now that you are here, shall we all take a stroll together along the river? The day is far too lovely to sit about when we may have a nice walk," Lady Diana proclaimed with her usual exuberance.

"If you care for a stroll, you may have one," the duke answered.

"That would be *splendid*," Lady Diana replied, and she walked arm-in-arm with him towards her mother, Isabella by her other side.

"Mother, we are to have a stroll along the river, isn't that ever so nice?" Lady Diana announced.

"I was going to suggest the very same thing. It is a lovely day, and I would enjoy nothing better than some light exercise. Mrs Price, Mr Price, will you accompany us?" the Duchess of Devonshire asked the older couple.

"Not me. You young folk go on and have your walk. It is a nice day for one, to be sure. I am going to make myself quite comfortable on this chair and watch the river go by while I think about fishing," the elderly gentleman said as he availed himself of a chair. Isabella could not help but smile, suspecting that Mr Price was relieved to have an opportunity to escape the party.

"I am not so old as to decline such a generous offer. I shall go, but I wish to walk beside Lady Diana," the thin, elderly woman answered as she looked at Isabella with a sprightly sort of expression, full of curiosity and warmth. "I shall enjoy a conversation with you, as well, if you would join me and Lady Diana while we stroll along the riverside on this beautiful day."

"I would like nothing better." Isabella smiled at the elderly woman.

"Oh, dear me, but you are dressed in black,

in mourning I understand. If you would rather remain behind, I cannot say I would find any fault in your decision."

"The exercise shall do me good, and as I am told by Lady Diana, I am in need of the good country air."

With Lady Diana in the middle and Mrs Price on the far side, the three set off leading the stroll, with the duchess and her son trailing a distance behind. Lady Diana walked at a lively pace and Mrs Price, who was far quicker than her years would suggest, had no trouble matching her stride. To Isabella's surprise, the stroll had become a brisk walk and she did not mind in the least. She enjoyed exercise, such as long walks and riding, and missed them exceedingly.

"Now that it is only us, we shall have a bit of gossip." The older woman laughed merrily, and she and Lady Diana chatted away about people whom they both obviously knew, but whom Isabella had not met. Not that she minded. She rather enjoyed the sound of their friendly chatter. It was comforting and amiable, and not taxing in the least.

They continued on as though they were near in age, and as if every manner of village gossip must be shared. It seemed that Mrs Price was interested in everything, and Isabella noticed that she was paying more attention to their conversation as it had taken on a more serious bent.

"What of His Grace? It has been a long time, but he still hardly ever invites anyone for dinners or teas. He hardly pays any social calls. I'm surprised to see him here today." Mrs Price glanced towards the sky, and then she looked back to Diana.

"I believe you may be right," Lady Diana answered.

"It is rather peculiar … but what is to be expected, the poor man? God save him … How sad for him, to have suffered such a terrible loss. But your brother, if I may say so, could have his choice of any woman he desired – or that is what I have heard. But he desires no one, does he?"

"He has sworn never to love again. He said that very thing many years ago."

"His heart is too broken." Mrs Price nodded to her young companion.

"My mother has taken pains to introduce him to suitable ladies, but he has not shown the slightest bit of interest. She has invited the daughters of dukes, of marquesses, and even a foreign princess to our estate."

"A princess, you say?"

"If anyone could win his heart, it would have been the princess. She was the picture of elegance. Her dresses were sewn in pearls and jewels. The extravagance of her gowns was so becoming on her. She had a nice figure, a fine bosom, and was as stylish as any woman I have ever seen. She had all the men enchanted, but even she could not turn *his* head."

Mrs Price nodded, a sad expression on her face. She turned to Isabella. "At least that is nothing you need be troubled by. You are an ethereal beauty. From what I have observed, you have a tiny waist and a well-formed figure. Poor Diana here, on the other hand ..."

Diana looked down on her own chest, shrugged her shoulders and, to everybody's surprise, giggled. "Oh, well. You are a good observer, Mrs Price. I may not have been blessed with a beautiful shape as other women have, but I have other qualities, at least that is what my mother always tells me."

Mrs Price gave Diana a cheerful, conspiratorial grin and patted her arm. "My dear, your dowry is one of those qualities."

"You are right about that, Mrs Price, right indeed." She smiled broadly, clearly restraining a fit of giggles. "Now, if you believe Isabella to be a beauty, wait until we see her in all the beautiful gowns that will accentuate her features even further. I wager she will turn any man's head, eligible or otherwise."

"Besides your brother's," Mrs Price said.

Isabella was shocked at Mrs Price's comment, never having considered herself a prospect for the duke – or the duke for her. However, she did her best not to reveal her surprise, and she ignored the comment.

"He is a lost cause, I am afraid." Diana gave a sigh. "I am inclined to consider him to be a solitary sort of man of late. He has not shown the slightest interest in becoming well acquainted with *any* woman," she said, and her expression turned from that of a person stating a series of facts, to a rather wide-eyed one.

"Why would he? He loved his wife with all that was in him," Mrs Price said. "Upon my word, their regard for each other was evident to all who knew them. From the time they met, it seemed that they shared a mutual admiration. They were first acquainted when they were younger than you are now. I tell you, it surprised no one that he married her. She made a lovely duchess; God rest her soul."

"Mrs Price, you astound me with your memory," Diana said, a slight tease in her voice.

"I have a memory that is surprising, even to me at times," the elderly lady replied earnestly, not having noticed Diana's teasing and un-aware of the humour in her own words. Instead, she returned to the subject. "I doubt he will ever recover. Seven years it has been, and he shows not a single sign of moving onwards. He is still a young man. I sometimes wonder if he does not feel any need to ..." She fell silent.

Isabella glanced at her companion in surprise, but Mrs Price appeared as innocent as a lamb. Isabella could not help but smile at her angelic facial expression, and she had to look away to hide her amusement. Her own father had explained the nature of the physical union between a man and a woman a long time ago. Indeed, he had found that on their travels, there were many things that he had to explain to Isabella that were not considered seemly for an innocent young woman to know, but which were essential for self-preservation, nonetheless.

"It *has* been seven years," Diana quickly said. "You are quite right. He remains as steely and stoic as ever, however, some things need time."

Isabella immediately noticed Diana's attempt at ending the topic and hoped Mrs Price understood.

"I believe you are quite right about him, my apologies to His Grace, I should say. It is not my place to speak of the duke as though I were his family. I most certainly am not. Nevertheless, I think you are not mistaken in believing that he could have any woman he wanted, even that foreign princess you spoke of."

Nobody gave an answer, which did not discourage Mrs Price from continuing her subject.

"If he wanted a wife, he would not hesitate, I am certain of that." She sighed. "He was always a wilful boy, and now he is just the same as a man. Heavens, but he knows his own mind, there can be no doubt." She peered behind her as if to confirm that he could not hear them. "His heart is broken, I fear, or so your mother, Her Grace, once told me. He is handsome, and his countenance is as comely as it has ever been, but there is sadness in his eyes."

Isabella did not dare turn around, but she

marked what Mrs Price and Lady Diana said in their discourse about the duke. She recalled what she knew of the manner in which the dowager duchess spoke to her son, and she came to the conclusion that the woman must be in agreement with the opinions shared by her daughter and Mrs Price. The duke was a stern man, and a heartbroken one, which she presumed accounted for his coldness. Isabella felt some of her less-than-charitable emotions softening inside her, and she considered adopting a more empathetic attitude towards His Grace.

Her experience of the gentleman had been that the duke was not an intolerant man, nor was he cruel, rather he was distant and did not display any emotion. In the opinion she had formed upon her arrival, and which had re-mained unaltered for the most part since – he was incapable of love or of feeling any emotion other than loyalty to his mother and to his title. What of the matter of his broken heart? He could and would not love anyone. *How terrible,* she thought.

As they continued their walk along the river, Isabella could not resist the pull of curiosity any longer. Glancing behind her, she studied the duke. His gaze was fixed firmly on the river, but she doubted he was watching the water as it flowed past them. She also suspected that he was far from the ongoing conversation of his mother, who was at his side speaking to him. Was he thinking of his wife, a woman whom he had lost seven years ago?

He raised his head towards her, and their eyes met just as that thought came to her. For a brief moment, she felt as if he could read it plainly on her face – or perhaps in her mind. For in that short second, that somehow seemed to last much longer, she felt as if she had been granted a brief glimpse into his soul and he into hers. However, even as she began to redden, he turned his gaze back to the water as though he had not even noticed her.

Looking down at her black dress, which marked her as different among the women on the village green, who were all wearing bright whites, pale pinks, and greens, Isabella decided that as soon as she could manage, she would begin to search in earnest for a husband or a situation which would allow her to leave the duke's residence. She had no wish to burden him any more than he burdened himself. From the expression on his face, she knew that he did not require a single additional responsibility or duty. She also reasoned that he did not care to add anyone else to his set of close acquaintances or give any thought to a person such as herself, who might seek his good opinion. If he wished to be alone in his sorrow, then she did not intend to disturb him while he mourned his departed wife in his own solitary manner any longer than was necessary.

She felt grateful that he agreed to offer her a home and lodging at all, and she decided that if a match could not be found, she would advertise in the hope of finding an arrangement among good and respectable people. Yes, she vowed to herself – that would be the end of the debt he was paying. He would no longer owe her father or her anything further. He could return to his estate and business, and Isabella would not trouble him further. Deep in thought as she was, Isabella did not overhear the conversation that was taking place behind her. It was a conversation that she would have found most interesting, if she had heard even a sentence of it.

THE DISCUSSION between the duke and his mother was the reason he was staring into the waters of the river, and his expression was as far away as he wished he could be. His mother, being the person she was, had taken the opportunity to – yet again – chide him about his current unmarried state. It was a common occurrence but one that annoyed him exceedingly, although it was to be endured. She was his mother, and she had assumed her former responsibilities as duchess without complaint. Therefore, he could not, and would not, treat her with anything other than respect, even if that did not alter his private opinion. Her not-so-subtle censure was based on her keen observation – she was certain that she detected something in his manner that had changed.

It was this statement that something about him had changed that had sent the duke into a deeply reflective state, as he walked along the river – the same river that flowed through his estate and the one where he had first met John Thornton many years earlier. He had saved Georgiana's dog from this river, a memory which led him back to Georgiana, as his thoughts often turned to her. Memories of his wife flooded back into his mind as rapidly as the water flowing in the river. They were inescapable. The images of her, and of their happy days together were always a torment, as much as he wished it were otherwise.

His mother's frequent criticism of him for not remarrying did nothing to further her cause, no matter which wealthy young woman she championed. As his mother continued to speak ceaselessly about the matter, he considered telling her that her methods – and her opinions – were not endearing the idea of marriage to him. If he did ever remarry, it would be as a necessity and that would be all that he could offer anyone foolish enough to accept his proposal. The very thought of any woman taking his wife's place had been abhorrent since her death. Nonetheless, that judgement had slowly and gradually changed from one of abhorrence, into a display of the respect for the woman he called wife.

Georgiana had been a singular woman. She had deserved the love he felt for her when she wore the title of Duchess, as well as the continued regard he held for her all these years after her death. Her confidence, cleverness, aristocratic demeanour, and beauty were unmatched when she was yet alive. As a memory, she had become more idealised. He knew with certainty, that his mother was mistaken if she presumed that any woman living in England could equal his duchess. In his memory, Georgiana was perfect. It was not guilt or disloyalty which stayed his hand and his heart from loving another woman, it was the supreme confidence that he had loved the best of women, and no one could compare to her, either in wit, or ability. His mother had been a formidable and well-respected duchess in her youth, and his wife was just as venerable. It would require a woman of remarkable skill and accomplishment to deserve the title, a title that no amount of beauty and elegance could purchase. A duchess in his estimation was not a countess or a marchioness, but carried the burden of highest rank among women, and was surpassed by few in the realm. With that certainty, he endured his mother's prattle about remarriage, as he often did, appearing to listen but silently confident in his own decision. A decision he had no intention of altering in any way.

Unknown to Mrs Price, as she continued to

speak of the duke and his lost love in hushed tones, her observation of the current state of the duke was quite accurate. With a knowing nod of her head, the older woman insisted rather emphatically:

"Mark my words, these are the thoughts of an old woman who has seen a great many things in her life – and remembers them all. His Grace, God save him, shall *never* remarry." She sighed and looked at Isabella.

"Lady Isabella, if you had been acquainted with his dear departed wife, you would under-stand the reason for his sorrow. Never before or since has such a woman graced our village. Lady Diana will agree, and so must every other soul who knew the duchess, that she was the kind of woman a man would never forget. It is terribly tragic but there is nothing to be done for it, nothing at all. The duke, despite his title and grand houses, shall never love again, he has sworn it … and I believe it!"

CHAPTER 7

*I*sabella sat in her dark raven-like clothes. Once again, she imagined herself as one of the black birds that were ever present in the English countryside. She knew that she must remain clothed as she was for two more months, before she could even consider wearing a single frock from the new clothes that the Duchess of Devonshire had ordered for her.

Isabella did not begrudge the respect that she owed to her father. She missed him sorely and still lamented his passing every day. It was the knowledge that she was unable to search for a situation, including a betrothal while she mourned him, that frustrated her. Her despondency was beginning to give way to an increasing urgency to no longer be a burden on His Grace. She could wait two months, but did she wish to remain a day longer? She sighed. The dowager duchess had also noticed Isabella's listless demeanour. She signalled her concern by not-so-surreptitious glances at Isabella, as she entertained a group of women who had come to call on a foggy, misty day in autumn.

The conversation had turned, as it often did, to gossip from the neighbouring villages and the county. Isabella was not so inclined to speak her opinions or to add anything to the discourse, but she did listen on occasion to the subjects that were discussed. Even as she was becoming aware that she was slipping into the role of a tragic figure in the background.

A cup of tea sat in her hand, as she stared out of the window of the drawing room. The trees were no longer as brightly green or as lush as they had been in the summertime. Now, their leaves were golden, with sprays of red and orange that hinted at the coming chill. She could already feel coldness seeping into the great house, as stealthily as the light mist crept upon the hills outside.

The conversation in the drawing room continued on, and she listened half-heartedly as she had other thoughts to occupy her mind. As her eyes swept the gardens listlessly, she suddenly became aware of a male figure standing there. She stared in shock and her eyes widened before she froze. It was … *him.* It was her half-brother! He had found her! How had he found her? She stumbled backwards from the window, but she could not remove her gaze from the man she had hoped never to face again.

However, she soon realised that she might have been mistaken. *It was* not *her half-brother,* she told herself to calm her racing heart, but she could not say, not with certainty. Night *was* drawing in, and while it was not completely dark out, the weather was grey, and the evening was advanced enough to make it hard to distinguish anyone's features at this distance. Closer scrutiny revealed a sturdily built, well-dressed young gentleman, with similar attributes to her half-brother – probably an acquaintance of the family whom she had not yet met, she reasoned. She saw him gesture casually to a dog that she had not noticed until then, and she saw a carriage was standing nearby. Still shaken by the shock, her eyes followed the gentleman and his black dog, as they walked towards the coach, the dog stopping to sniff here and there along the way. Just before the man climbed into his carriage, he turned and gazed in her direction. Isabella instinctively took a step aside, removing herself from the window. Had he seen her staring at him? For a few seconds, she held her breath. No, the lamps had not yet been lit in the room, so she was most likely invisible from the outside, behind the glossy surface of the glass. She slowly moved her head back to the window. Peering out, the last thing she saw was his carriage moving off.

Isabella felt a flood of relief, and it took a moment for her to regain her composure.

"My dear, you appear wan. Are you unwell?" the Duchess of Devonshire asked as soon as there was not a single guest left in the drawing room. She and her daughter had bidden their guests goodbye, sending them out into the chilly autumn evening.

Isabella had noticed that she had been the subject of the older woman's regard, even if it had only been fleeting. The subsequent observation was not surprising, but Isabella did not wish to speak of her despair. Looking from Lady Diana to the duchess, she knew that she would be unable to escape their good intentions or their insistence that the subject be broached. Setting her teacup carefully on its saucer, she tried to adopt a light-hearted façade.

"It must be the weather. Dreary days do nothing to help me forget my sorrow."

"Today may be dreary, but there won't always be dreary days, not when we arrive in London!" Lady Diana chimed in, her concern reverting to her usual charming optimism. "There will be a ball, you must know that. A ball, given for us. It will be such fun to be presented together. Side by side, as if we were sisters."

"That is an occasion I am earnestly anticipating," Isabella answered.

The dowager duchess smiled as she regarded Isabella. "How I remember my first season in London ... the handsome young men in their finery. Officers in their crimson regimentals ... many of whom wanted to pay calls on me. I was fortunate to be a lady of a noble family, in possession of a dowry and accomplishments." Her lips curved as she glanced towards Isabella. "That is what makes a season a success, you must know. I am sure yours will be a momentous time, marked by many invitations to dine and attend balls. You may look forward to introductions to eligible young men. I am confident that you will make the most of the opportunities that come your way, a certainty for a young lady, such as yourself."

"I must confess that I feel rather nervous about it," Isabella admitted.

"Isabella. Let no one tell you that you are not a beauty. You possess a countenance that is pleasing and fair … but are you prepared to put forth your talents to be admired or criticised? Beauty shall win you notice, but your accomplishments shall prove your education and breeding."

"My skills may not be what they ought–"

"What do accomplishments mean to a young man who may fall in love with you?" Lady Diana exclaimed teasingly and gazed dreamily into space.

"Daughter, you will not have to concern yourself with your accomplishments provided they are adequate, something which I have taken pains to ensure they are, as befits the daughter of a duke," the dowager duchess replied. "I have no wish to embarrass our guest by a discussion regarding financial matters and dowries – but without an established number of properties, demonstrable talent and beauty *will* win the day. It is unappetising to discuss money, but I am afraid it cannot be avoided. A fine display of skills will undoubtedly be of great importance, when little else can be offered."

"I am the daughter of an Earl … is that not of some importance, at least?" asked Isabella.

The Duchess of Devonshire lowered her voice as if she was addressing a subject she found distasteful. "My dearest Isabella, I wish it *were* of the greatest importance, but you have to consider the facts. I do not wish to cause you offense. Let me explain." The duchess took a sip of her tea before she continued, "In London, where there are young ladies of noble houses, in possession of beauty, accomplishments, and dowries, you shall find yourself set against them in a vulgar sort of competition. The style of your dresses, which Diana and I have taken care to ensure are among the finest and most fashionable, shall be noticed at once. As will your skills in the art of conversation, music, drawing, and your deportment. I have observed, my dear, that you carry yourself with an aristocratic air. Your posture and bearing are as they should be, but what of your ability to play music or draw? In London, you will find opportunities to display all those talents, and they shall mark you out as worthy of a gentleman's attention. Dancing and music are easily studied, and you can be considered a competent singer if you are not gifted in the playing of music. Dancing is similar in that you may prove yourself up to the task, with a minimum of effort spent. That is, assuming you have had instruction in the arts required of a lady?"

"I do not think I have heard you practice," Lady Diana said. "Is your playing sufficient, and what of your singing? Are you talented in that area? I am sure that you must have enjoyed instruction from as many as I did."

"My instruction was not as consistent as yours, to be certain," Isabella replied. "My father taught me many details of art and architecture, which I am pleased to know about. I was versed in the usual sources of literature and history, and mathematics. My geography is not lacking, and my languages are passable. The instructions that I received may not have been as I would have wished – but I have travelled."

"What of your musical instruction?" The dowager duchess asked, her stare quite direct.

"I am not *un*skilled, if that is what you mean," answered Isabella hesitantly, her cheeks flushing red.

"Come, come, my dear," the dowager duchess said as she poured another cup of tea. "My interest is not in humiliating you. Quite the opposite is true. I wish to learn whether there are any deficiencies apparent in your education, while we have time to ensure that these are not allowed to embarrass you in the drawing rooms of London."

"I will confess that my education has not always been consistent."

The duchess nodded her head as if she had not expected a different answer. "While you have been in mourning, I have been as respectful of that as I can, and have allowed you a reasonable amount of time to grieve, however, now I feel it is time I ask you this question. Would it be kind of me to allow you to venture to London to be presented and then humiliated when you are asked to play, sing, or ride? For the sake of you and your father, whom I knew when he was a young gentleman, I feel it is incumbent upon me to see that you are prepared for what may await you." The dowager duchess took another sip of her tea.

Isabella understood and was grateful to the older woman. Lady Diana offered encouragement. "You are so clever, even if you are not as well educated as I am. You are in possession of attributes which cannot be taught by tutors, is she not, Mother?"

"Diana, please watch your manners," the duchess chided her daughter.

She looked back towards Isabella. "As I

stated earlier, your carriage and bearing are as they should be for a woman of your background. Possibly more than they ought. You could never be mistaken for a commoner, not with your confident manner and air. I will have Diana see to your music, if you wish to practice. What of your riding? I cannot overstate the importance of equestrian skills for a woman who may become the mistress of an historic estate one day."

"Riding? In London? It would be wonderful..." Isabella said.

The older woman raised her hand slightly, causing Isabella to pause in her sentence. "You may demonstrate your skills by riding in the park, but I hardly think it seemly. Carriage rides will do for a young woman in the capital. However, it is by attending hunting parties and being invited to country estates that you will be given the opportunity to prove your skills as a horsewoman. A skill, which may be viewed as essential depending on which gentleman considers you as a potential wife."

"Perhaps, my riding skills could use improvement. I enjoy riding, but I am not as experienced as I may be," Isabella admitted. "I do not wish to be a burden, not when my own skills are adequate. I have no wish to incur any further debt to His Grace. You are not suggesting incurring any more expenses on my behalf, are you?" Isabella spoke candidly, more candidly than she may have wished, but her answer was sincere.

The duchess answered while stirring the tea in her cup quite vigorously, "My dear, I have never been concerned for expenses. I consider the question of it to be unseemly for a lady. Still, I cannot fault you for your concern. It is a mark of your independent nature that you have no wish to be indebted – a remarkable trait in a woman and more so when I think of your age. However, I give you my personal assurance that money and the paying of wages does not enter into the discussion when it comes to riding. My son is unparalleled in his ability with a horse. If there is anyone who is in possession of the skills necessary to ensure your reputation as a competent horsewoman, it shall be him and no one else. I shall see to it that he takes charge of assessing and improving your equestrian abilities."

Isabella swallowed.

"My brother is a splendid rider, in fact, the best in this part of the country," Lady Diana chimed in again, as was her habit, giving Isabella no time to protest. "He loves nothing better than an afternoon riding across the hills and dales. If you have not a riding habit of your own, you may have mine for the asking. But Mother, is it in accordance with mourning? It will do you no end of good, say what you will."

"There is no question to be asked. Mourning will not keep you from your studies and your skills as a lady," the duchess answered, and then she looked at Isabella and smiled warmly. "You will be an accomplished woman when you are presented. Your accomplishments will elevate your beauty and grace enormously. You will be a sensation; I am sure of it.

I have no concern for my Diana, you see. Her dowry and her title will see her through, but you, my dear, you shall be admired for your skills and your pleasant features. I shall see to it personally. Accompany Diana to her room – a riding habit must be fitted."

Lady Diana was on her feet, holding out her hand to Isabella as she beamed. "It is exciting, is it not? I shall inform my brother at once."

Isabella felt helpless to say no to the generosity of her two benefactresses (neither of whom was going to be saddled, strictly speaking, with her instruction on horseback). As she allowed herself to be pulled up the stairs of the enormous house, she wanted to protest, but, how could she? Lady Diana and her mother wished to do all they could to assist her. Their intentions were honest and open. There was not the slightest hint of malice about them. For now, she was doing what she had to, until she could manage to free herself from her debt to the duke and his family. Until then, she was compelled to accept their help, at least until she arrived in London. Considering their charitable natures, she could not help but stop and wonder about the person who would give her instructions.

Had His Grace been consulted regarding this scheme, and what would *his* reaction be?

CHAPTER 8

*A*s she stood in the stable, a building that was as grandly constructed as the house, Isabella realised she had not been alone with the duke since the night of her arrival. His Grace was a tall, broad-shouldered man, and not gaunt – on the contrary, she observed. He was powerfully built, so much so that she could not help but be reminded of the strength that radiated from him. When mounted, he would surely have a potential for speed and force that was breath-taking. Swathed in the black material of his coat and hat, Matthew Danvers, the

Duke of Devonshire, strode out with a confidence that could be interpreted as arrogance. He moved with the ease and freedom of a man who was accustomed to being in complete control (and at all times). She had not noticed that conceit, that certainty and prowess before, as she had not been alone with him for any amount of time that might allow the observation of these traits. Other things she had not been able to observe were his deep-brown eyes, and the lightness of his hair, as well as the scowl – a perpetual feature of his face – which softened into a thin line, showing neither joy nor disgust.

If she were forced to speculate, she would guess that he was not pleased with his additional task. However, his accession to his mother's and sister's wishes showed that he could be loyal. Even as Isabella knew that he would have undoubtedly refused, had the request for riding instruction emanated from anyone but his own sister.

Standing in a borrowed riding habit in the

stables and looking up at the duke who met her gaze with his own, she was struck by a surge of self-consciousness. That awareness did not stem from embarrassment or weakness, but from the thought of a confession she had not made to Lady Diana, for fear of shocking her. Diana was a sweet girl, but she was decidedly traditional when it came to matters of women and their adherence to convention. Isabella had understood before this moment, that she had been raised in an eccentric fashion, and that her education was somewhat eclectic. In all her years, the question of her equestrian skills had never been broached until this very moment.

She raised her head and fixed her gaze upon his, her blue eyes meeting the impenetrable stare of his dark-brown ones. Isabella prepared herself for the inevitable confession. It was a moment that she knew was coming quickly.

"Lady Isabella, my groom has saddled my sister's horse for your use. You will find the mare is reliable and docile," he said as he gestured towards the dappled mare waiting by her stall. "I have every confidence that she will suit you. If you are prepared to mount the horse, we shall be on our way."

The cool air of the autumn afternoon did nothing to ease Isabella's discomfort. She felt warmth, a heat rising to her cheeks. There was no reason for such a reaction, but she was powerless to stop it. She felt his scrutiny growing more intense, and his agitation becoming more apparent the longer she stood without making a move towards the horse.

"Are you waiting for me to inspect the animal, to give you my approval?" she asked.

"Your approval? I consider that to be unnecessary. A stable boy will assist you to mount the horse if you require it."

"What is the horse's name?" Isabella asked, stalling for time as she looked at the animal.

"Athena," he answered. "You may call her that or any other name you care to use."

"Athena ... that is a lovely name. The mare is named after the Greek goddess of wisdom, if I am not mistaken. I sincerely hope the horse has the wisdom to see me safely returned to the stables after our ride."

"Take your place on the saddle, and we shall see who possesses the necessary wisdom to accomplish a canter along the hills. If you will be so kind as to mount the horse?"

"Yes, yes, mount the horse, I will do that," Isabella answered as she studied the animal. The horse was a gentle creature, probably a fine fit for his sister, who was also sweet-natured and kind. She observed that feature of the animal from its big brown eyes, but there was a difficulty and one she wished was surmountable, but it was not.

"Lady Isabella?" the duke said.

Isabella could plainly see that she was not to escape her circumstances, as unusual as they were. Her confession could not be delayed any longer.

"Your Grace," she began.

"Yes, Lady Isabella, what is it?" he asked, his impatience evident.

"The horse is a fine one, she looks sweet-tempered," Isabella said. "I realise I should have spoken sooner, but your sister and your mother have a way of being rather … persuasive. They were insistent yesterday that I go riding."

He gave a short smile. "I agree. They can be insistent upon a great many things. What is concerning you? Do you not ride? Have you not had any experience at all?"

"You may very well wish to go without me," she said. "Forgive me, Your Grace, but I have no wish to bother you. You see, I am a competent rider, better than most, I would dare say."

"Then, what concerns you? Is the horse not wild enough for a rider of your skill?" he asked, a lilt of condescension in his voice.

"She will do, there is no question of that. I prefer a mount to have a demeanour like my own, and I shall be glad of her gentleness and your selection of her – when you hear what I have yet to disclose to you. Indeed, I may be rather grateful for a gentle animal beneath me before our ride is at an end. I should have spoken plainly to your sister, but I am not accustomed to riding as a lady would. I was taught to ride astride."

"Astride?" he asked, his eyebrow raised in a question, at the same time as his lips curved into a smirk.

"Astride, Sir. You have heard me correctly. Astride as *you* might ... as a man would ride a horse. In my own defence, I hasten to say that it is not at all uncommon in the New World, where I did most of my early riding."

"You have travelled to the New World?" The duke appeared as astonished as if she had just confessed to having travelled to the moon.

"Yes, Sir," she replied. "My father managed to retain land in Virginia, even after the king lost a great deal of his to the new union. We spent many happy months there together, and it was not at all unusual for women to ride astride. Given the sometimes-raw nature of the colonies, I believe it to have been the most expedient method for all. In that manner, I should offer any man able competition. Side-saddle, I fear, I may be clumsy and fall from the mount."

"You astonish me," was all the Duke of Devonshire could manage as he gestured for a stable boy.

The stable boy, a young man not many years younger than herself, aided Isabella onto the horse. She was thankful that she did not fall, nearly as much as she was to the horse who appeared to understand that the woman who was on its back was not at all comfortable seated in a side-saddle, her leg looped over the horn. Fortunately, Isabella was confident about her ability to ride, even if she was less than certain about the manner in which she was seated.

The duke, as Isabella expected, rode Trapper, the powerful stallion who matched his master in both pride and disposition. Leaving the stables, she followed him until they reached the road leading past the gardens and proceeded to go out onto the dales.

Under the shade of a tree with leaves of a golden-amber hue, he stopped, and she slowed Athena beside him. Her horse appeared to be particularly docile in the presence of Trapper.

"I see you are still upon Athena," he observed. "She has exhibited the good wisdom not to send you flailing into the dirt."

"The good wisdom, or perhaps it is her kind nature," Isabella replied. "I believe that she has taken pity upon me, Sir. She is as merciful and generous as her mistress."

"A wise choice," he said.

Isabella wondered if the duke was referring to his choice of horse for her or the horse's choice in not sending her flying from its back. Before she could reply to either option, he tipped his hat to her and continued, "Will you excuse us for a few minutes?" He gave her a smile – a real and genuine smile – such as she had not even suspected he had in him. It transformed his entire face into a visage that was as handsome and dashing as any she had ever beheld. Then, he spurred his horse and he was gone.

She watched, entranced by the sight of the duke galloping down the lane astride his swift and powerful horse. Trapper's legs stretched out, and his muscles rippled in effort, whereas the duke appeared to be as comfortable on his back as he was in the wing-backed chair in his study, or perhaps more so. Urging her own mount forward, albeit slowly, she felt the animal's hesitation.

Tearing her eyes away from the sight of Trapper and his master vanishing down the dirt road, Isabella whispered to the horse beneath her, "There, there, Athena, we do not have to keep their pace. If the gentlemen wish to be silly, they can do as they please while *we* will be ladies."

Isabella did not truly believe that the horse understood her words, but she was inclined to think that Athena was soothed by the calming tone of her voice. The mare walked forward and then slowly picked up her pace. It was not an alarming speed, but it was enough to signal to Isabella that she wished to catch up to Trapper, even if she did not want to gallop. Isabella was uncertain in the side-saddle, and she tried to recall what she knew of riding in that position. She was careful not to make any mistakes or to relax too much. Oh, if only she could ride as she wished! She could have easily caught Trapper by now, but she dared not urge Athena to go faster – not until she was certain of her bearing and confident that she would not fall and break her neck.

The duke, who was now a small figure in the distance, turned and urged Trapper to gallop back towards her. As he approached, she saw that he was wearing an unfamiliar and broad smile. His eyes were sparkling, and his features were shaped into an expression of sublime contentment. Slowing to a trot and then a walk, Trapper shook his mane exuberantly – he almost seemed as pleased as his master.

"What a show, Sir! Trapper is a magnificent animal and you handle him well," Isabella said with a smile.

"He is, without a doubt, the best horse in my stable," the Duke of Devonshire replied as he affectionately patted the horse. "I am pleased you did not try to hasten after us. Trapper enjoys a good gallop, and he needs a spirited ride to blow off the stable cobwebs, but we shall not leave you behind again. Eh, old boy?" He patted the horse on the neck affectionately.

"We would never be offended by your choosing to enjoy a gallop across the dales. The weather is perfect for a ride today. Athena and I shall just amble along."

"I have given my word that I shall give you instruction," he said.

"You mean, improve my ability to ride side-saddle. Astride, and with the right horse, I could easily have been your equal in speed just now. I may not have surpassed you, but I would have been at your side." Isabella gave him a challenging expression.

"I believe that you would have been up to the task," the duke replied jovially and without hesitation, "but not many gentlemen"–he caught himself–"British gentlemen would appreciate that particular talent. Indulge me, ride ahead. I wish to see how you carry yourself."

Isabella did as she was bid, riding ahead and

aware of his eyes on her. How altered he seemed today, when he was away from his house and the duties of his title! He had smiled as Isabella had not thought possible a mere day before. His transformation was as remarkable as the obviously deep affection he held for his horse.

"Lady Isabella," he said as he reached her side. Trapper whickered softly also as if to greet Athena. "Your carriage is correct, but you are leaning entirely too much to one side."

Isabella nodded. "Oh, I suppose I am over-compensating my balance."

"Hold yourself erect, adjust your hips, if you permit me to be so indelicate."

"Do not concern yourself with indelicacy. Say what you mean if you must, I am not the fainting variety," she answered truthfully (well, not completely truthfully) as she adjusted her posture and her hips. Isabella's heartbeat *had* increased when she had felt the duke's eyes on her figure.

"There, I have made alterations – what is your pronouncement?"

"Sit back in the saddle, along your other side," he suggested confidently.

She sat back, straightened her shoulders.

"Yes, that is better. You should now feel more secure in the seat."

"That *is* better. I do not feel as though I may slip and injure myself," she replied, but more shyly than before.

"Shall we ride, Lady Isabella? A canter perhaps, so you can get the measure of the gait?"

"A canter would be enjoyable – it will give me an opportunity to test my balance, if that is what I must do to catch a husband!" It was an attempt at humour (mostly to help overcome her lingering self-consciousness), said lightly. She did not wait for him to answer. Instead, she urged her horse forward as the track broadened out.

Athena pricked up her ears as if to indicate that she felt the renewed confidence that flowed from her young rider, and Isabella gave herself up to the moment. She forgot her previous lack of confidence and her feelings of being an unskilled horsewoman, as Athena's strides lengthened, and the mare switched into a gentle rolling canter along the green path.

The sun was shining, peeking out from behind a few white, wispy clouds as she sat back and enjoyed the scenery before her. The estate of Hardwick Manor truly was breath-taking – rolling hills surrounded the house, and trees and streams bordered long expanses of meadows and fields. The stone cottages of tenants and farmers dotted the landscape, creating vignette-like images such as she had seen in bucolic country scenes in paintings. The breeze, a warm one for that time of year, was pleasant. She glanced up, savouring the warmth upon her face. She saw the duke turn towards the sun similarly, an expression of supreme contentment on his handsome face.

She was reminded that he was a man, not just a duke, and an imposingly powerful figure.

He was a man, who had suffered loss and whose heart had hardened.

Riding at his side, both of them smiling and laughing, it was easy to forget such matters as finding a husband or seeking a position as a governess. Today was simply too beautiful and the company too agreeable to reflect upon her sorrow or her restlessness regarding her prospects. Today, as she looked at her companion and enjoyed herself, she could imagine that her life was carefree. From the duke's demeanour, she guessed that she was not the only person on their ride who was enjoying the outing.

Her happy thoughts and the contentment of the day were interrupted by her horse, of all things. The creature suddenly slowed to a trot, unexpectedly. Isabella tightened her grip on the reins and the muscles in her thighs as she tried to remain seated. The horse slowed to a walk, and her gait was no longer fluid. Isabella realised that something was amiss.

"Athena, stop, and we shall have a good look

at you. Are you injured? Have I asked too much of you, dear girl?"

"Has your horse gone lame?" the duke asked as he slowed to meet her pace.

"I cannot say … something has happened, although I know not what."

"There is a stream ahead, we should halt there. The horses can drink, and we can attend to Athena." The duke gestured towards a green clearing that lay ahead.

Isabella nodded in agreement, patting the horse, and soothing her with her voice as they came to a halt. Realising the need for an ungraceful dismount, Isabella prepared herself to jump down – as soon as she was able to untangle herself and her long skirt from the side-saddle.

However, she found the duke beside her horse, his hands reaching towards her as he said: "Permit me."

"Thank you, Your–" she answered as she slid off of the horse, feeling his strong hands catching her waist before she fell the entire way. With her feet firmly on the ground, she was aware that she was looking into his eyes. She was close to him, her back against Athena, her hands on his arms, and her breasts nearly touching his chest.

Breathlessly, she stood still, feeling his hands still on her waist, which was so small, his hands were nearly spanning it. Isabella's face was flushed from riding, or was it something else? His eyes were a deep brown, mysterious, and their depth was impossible to determine. She became lost in them, as she was in the moment. It was an unexpectedly intimate encounter with a man whose usual coldness did not extend to his touch. She felt the heat from his grip through the material of the riding jacket and did not know what to say. How was she to respond to him, and to his hands that *still* circled her waist? She had never been touched by a man in such a way. In fact, she had never been this close to any gentleman, apart from her dear papa. Certainly, her pulse had never raced like this because of a man.

"We should see to your horse," he said, his voice breaking the silence.

"Yes, we should," she answered, not wanting to move away. She was mesmerised by the feeling of his body so close to hers, his chest rising and falling with his breath, and with each drawn breath nearly touching hers. She did not move and neither did he, for how long she did not know, until, at last, her horse gingerly trod one step towards the stream, wanting to drink from it. The movement broke the spell that had fallen upon Isabella and the duke. She stared at his lips, so full and robust, like the rest of him. It seemed they were coming closer. Was he leaning *closer*?

"Lady Isabella?" His baritone voice was in her ears, the sound of it primal and male.

"Sir, forgive me …" she began, her heart beating against her ribs, and was at a loss for what to say after that. Forgive her – for what? For her thoughts that were running wild and free? She blushed a deep crimson.

He removed his hands from her waist. His

gaze was no longer intimate. He stared at her – his composure quickly returned to its usual coolness. As she studied him, she noticed that he had turned his attention away from her.

"Are you all right?" he asked in a manner that suggested politeness rather than concern.

"No, not at all, I mean – I apologize. I feel fine. My horse has gone lame, but I am unharmed. Possibly with the exception of my pride, which may have been injured as I tried to disengage my dress from that dreadful saddle." She became aware that she was talking too much, and that her voice was trembling.

"You were doing remarkably well. Your skill as a horsewoman is evident."

"I have my father to thank for that, as for all of my upbringing," she said. "I would not wish it to be any different, even if that option were available." It was as much an explanation of herself as of the freedom of her unusual homelife.

"I am aware of that," the duke replied reflectively, as he slowly bent to examine Athena's leg. Isabella knew that even the most experienced of riders could be injured approaching an animal that was lame or hurt, and she tried not to think of that as she watched him tend to the mare. She was riveted by the changed man she saw before her. A few hours ago, she could have sworn he saw her presence as only a burden. Yet, a mere minute ago, she had momentarily thought him as one of the amorous gentlemen she had read about in novels.

"Lady Isabella, she has a sharp stone in her hoof. It is no wonder she is favouring her other leg," he said in a soft tone of voice. "I fear the thing is tightly wedged. I worry I may cause her pain, or provoke an abscess, if I am too impatient in its removal."

Isabella approached Athena carefully, consciously attempting to compose herself. She feared that Athena, despite being a good-tempered mount, might lash out in her fear, and deliver a blow to the duke's head. Such a blow could kill. It was that remote danger that caused her to hold her breath. She did not want the horse to become skittish or nervous, if she sensed Isabella's own confusion or her tumbled feelings at that second. Athena needed a confident mistress – someone she could trust. Isabella was going to be that person, even if she did not feel that way after her brief encounter with the duke – an encounter that had taken her breath away, and which she scarcely understood.

"There, there, girl, I am here. You are well … everything is well." She soothed as she stroked the horse's mane.

Without waiting for any sign or indication that she should not, she began a soft, sweet song that her mother had sung to her when she was a child. It was an old Celtic lullaby. As she sang, she gently stroked the horse's face and nose. Trapper moved towards her as though he, too, was mesmerised by the singing (or so she hoped).

She watched the duke successfully remove the stone from the horse's hoof.

"There, the stone is out but it has left a small

open wound. I think it wise not to put any weight on the horse or risk any further injury. You may ride with me on Trapper, or we may walk if you so choose. I would send a carriage, but we are too far from any road."

"She is not permanently lame, is she?" Isabella asked, fearful of his answer. Lame horses served no purpose on an estate.

"She will be recovered in a day or two, but I do not want to cause her any unnecessary pain. Athena is my sister's horse, and I am certain my sister would wish her treated as well as possible. What shall it be: walking or riding?"

"We may walk, the distance is manageable," Isabella answered, declining his offer of riding as she did not dare to be close to him again. The closeness was not unpleasant, not at all, but she did not wish to experience any more confusion, especially after he had returned to his former, cold demeanour with abruptness. His smile and laugh were so distant a memory, that she wondered if she had dreamt all of it.

"As you wish," he answered as he left her side.

"Come along, Athena," she said and took hold of the reins, watching with disappointment as the duke walked ahead of her, Trapper at his side. He did not look back or speak to her for the rest of the afternoon. His behaviour, which she had considerable time to reflect upon, as they were a farther distance away from Hardwick Manor than she had first presumed, was more distant than before. And now he was silent, too! His disposition towards her made her wonder if she had imagined the spark she believed to have seen in his eyes when he had helped her down from the horse.

Recalling the words of Mrs Price, she knew the answer to the riddle of his coldness. She was certain that Mrs Price was right. *He shall never love again.* All the fear and uncertainty of the future returned to haunt her, as the sky overhead turned grey. Dark clouds were moving in, signalling bad weather. Looking at the overcast sky, which had been so blue mere moments ago, she could not help but compare the sky to her life.

Her prospects were as uncertain as the weather, and so she reconciled herself to her vow that she should leave Hardwick Manor as soon as she could manage. Staring at the duke's back, a man she had no hope of understanding, she was certain that leaving him to his duties was the only course available to her. A course she would be wise to accept sooner rather than later.

CHAPTER 9

"Mr Hayworth is here to see you, Your Grace," the footman said to Matthew as soon as he entered the house.

"Show him to my study," Matthew said as he hastened up the stairs.

Matthew was still wearing his riding attire. He was fresh from the ride with Isabella, when he was given the news that his solicitor was at Hardwick Manor. It was unusual for Mr Richard Hayworth to leave the city of London for any reason, and he had not done so for many years. His habits, like his nature, were consistent. This unexpected exodus from the city combined with his unannounced arrival was out of the ordinary. Matthew anticipated that events of some magnitude must have prompted the visit.

The duke was not prone to rushing or quickening his actions or his pace to suit anyone. However, it was his own impatience which was behind his desire to move quickly. His solicitor waited in his study. He had known him for a great many years and knew him to be a sober man, who was not given to impulse or spontaneity in any form. Yet, here he was at Hardwick Manor.

Matthew washed his hands and face. With his valet's assistance, he changed quickly from his riding attire. Resuming the unreadable visage he wore in the presence of his servants and men such as his solicitor, he composed himself. He was prepared to hear what the man had come to tell him.

"Mr Hayworth," he greeted the man who

was seated in the study. "A drink? Tea? You must be thirsty from your long journey."

"Nothing for me, thank you, Your Grace."

"As you wish. Shall we come to the reason for your visit?" Matthew said as he settled into his chair, an immense leather seat that had belonged to his father and his father before him. As he sat in this heavy piece of furniture, he stared at the balding round man across the desk. Mr Hayworth was nervous and fidgeting, which was not in the nature of the solicitor.

"Sir, it has been several weeks since you asked me to investigate the daughter of the Earl of Chatham," the solicitor began.

"It has been *months* – and it was not *her* that I wanted investigated, but her circumstances," Matthew corrected him as he folded his hands and stared at the man.

"Yes, Sir. I was mistaken on both counts. I misspoke, forgive me, for I have not had much rest. The journey was rather long, and I am fatigued. I came to speak to you personally when I learned of the news which I must impart to you. A letter would have been sufficient, but I dared not risk such correspondence being lost on the journey or being opened by anyone but Your Grace," he said, his face red, and his words pouring out of him.

Matthew could not recall ever having seen his solicitor acting so oddly or without his usual composure.

"Mr Hayworth. Perhaps you would care for a few minutes to compose yourself. Are you sure you are not in need of refreshment or rest? You are not acting like yourself."

Nodding his round head vigorously the other man agreed, "You are quite right. I am not at all acting like myself. If I may begin again?"

"Take the time that you require," Matthew answered.

"Thank you."

Taking a few deep breaths, Mr Hayworth's shoulders heaved as though he carried a great burden. He wiped his face with the handkerchief that he withdrew from his waistcoat.

"I am embarrassed that you should see me in this state. I beg for your indulgence and that you will not alter your opinion of me ... or my work ... or my firm, for that matter, based on any deficiencies in character which I am undoubtedly exhibiting."

"Not at all. Whenever you are ready to begin."

"I am ready. I shall begin, with your permission, Sir, and with the reason, no, the necessity for my travelling to your estate without announcement. There was not sufficient time to write a letter, and I did not dare risk it arriving and falling into the wrong hands, as I have stated, even in error."

"The wrong hands?" the duke asked, his curiosity piqued. "My servants are not lapse in their duties. Am I to understand that there is another reason for your concern for the proper delivery of letters in my household?"

"It concerns Lady Isabella. I have been thorough in my research of her circumstances. They are most grave indeed. I find myself even feeling some sympathy for her and her plight. It is my regard for her and her security that has brought me to you."

The duke's curiosity was more than piqued now, as he studied the solicitor, who seemed to be regaining his usual steady composure. Matthew wanted to know more, but he resigned himself to being patient.

"Pray, continue."

"I know that my exhaustion and lack of food must be the cause of my thinking which does not seem rational. I shall begin in a different way. I will dispel any doubts or concerns that you may have and answer your questions – the same questions that you dispatched to me when you were made aware of the death of Lady Isabella's father, the Earl of Chatham. I shall speak to you about her half-brother, the heir to the title. He is the natural son of the Earl of Chatham and his first wife, who died when the boy was born."

Matthew nodded subtly. "Her half-brother, the Viscount of Pellington, Charles Thornton? I imagine he has assumed the title of my departed friend?"

"Yes, Lord Pellington is the heir apparent, although there has been some concern raised over his inheritance of the title. An impediment has arisen that has delayed the usual course of succession."

"An impediment? Charles Thornton is the legal heir to the title and the estates. He is the sole son and the heir to the title of the Earl of Chatham, is he not?"

"He *is* the direct male descendent and by right should inherit the title and all of the estate as it is entailed, Sir, but in spite of that, recent developments have cast some doubt on to the legality of his claim to the inheritance and the title. There has also been ample cause for concern regarding the personal safety of Lady Isabella."

"Her safety. How so? I must admit I have been puzzled about why Lady Isabella's father would entrust her welfare to me, when she possesses a half-brother who could see to her care.

I understand she is related, however distantly, to a well-placed cousin, the Viscount of Wharton on her mother's side of the family."

"Her cousin may be the Viscount of Wharton, but with the death of her mother, that connection – it was already strained if I may say so – has become untenable. Regarding the impediment, I fear that it is most grave. It comes not as a result of legal issues or any opposition to the inheritance, nor is it due to the structure of the will. His Lordship's will was quite clear. Given his immense wealth, he did make provisions for his daughter, but it was clearly his son who stood to inherit his title and the whole of the estate. As I have said, there was an exception made for an amount outside of the estate that was to be settled on Lady Isabella for her use as a dowry, and any expenses she might incur until the time of her marriage. The whole of the former Earl's business holdings and property comprised that entailment. It was to have been inherited by her half-brother, the Honourable Charles Thornton, Viscount of

Pellington, but his actions and the suspicions that were raised caused the entailment of the title and the settlement of the will to be halted until further investigation could be conducted when he was found."

"What evidence is necessary to settle a legally disputed title?"

"Evidence regarding his innocence must be presented, Sir. If I may speak in confidence … I fear that Lady Isabella would be overwhelmed with grief and fear if the details of her brother's charges should become known."

"Go on, you have yet to inform me of any wrongdoing that would warrant a delay in the transmission of his title and his lands."

"I have learned," began the solicitor as he instinctively lowered his voice, and leaned close to the desk, "Of a terrible argument that occurred between the viscount and his half-sister not long before the earl's death. The viscount has never cared for his half-sister. On the contrary, he holds Lady Isabella to account for a crime of which she is blameless."

"His own mother died at his birth, and the earl married again, when the boy was around eight years old. The child was fortunate and developed a tender, mother-son relationship with the earl's second wife, who I understand cared for him deeply."

"Her own daughter was born much later, when the young viscount was almost a man. The family were in the Indies overseeing the management of a new hill station, and the earl's wife and her daughter – two years old at the time – both contracted scarlet fever. The child survived but the mother did not. The viscount was at boarding school in England at the time, so he was spared. However, upon learning of that lady's death, he turned against his half-sister."

"Do we know why he turned against her?" the duke asked.

"It would appear that he blamed his half-sister for bringing disease into the house, and thus he believed she caused the death of his beloved stepmother."

"Her father must have been aware of this discord among his children."

"The earl was aware of it, but he was powerless to ease his son's terrible distress, or to dissuade him that his half-sister was responsible for his stepmother's death. It was a death that the young man never recovered from. It has been suggested that he was a rebellious youth, dissolute in his habits, and this worsened after the death of the earl's second wife. Those habits contributed to his anger and his vexation and … I dare say his spending. He gambled away vast sums of money, losing a fortune as his love of drink grew and prodigious amounts were added to his debts. These facts cannot be disputed, unfortunately as his debts are well-documented in his circle."

Mr Hayworth paused for a moment and then continued in the tone of one who was reluctant to follow bad news with speculation, "There are also rumours, which cannot be substantiated, as yet …but I heard tales that he is also involved in an inappropriate *liaison* with a woman, who has left her fiancé for him. There is even talk of a possible child, but as I say, I have no proof of that. As you know people do love to see further sin, after bad living has made itself at home. I might add that my source was not the most reliable."

Matthew considered the words of his solicitor as he studied the man. He trusted him implicitly. He considered the information would be treated with discretion when he spoke. "Lady Isabella has not mentioned her half-brother to me at all, nor, I believe, to my sister or mother."

"I would be astonished if she wished to be reminded of him," was Mr Hayworth's immediate reply. "He remained in London for most of her life, while she accompanied her father on his journeys all over the world. It was not until her father's illness and his return to England that she encountered the viscount again. By all accounts it was not a happy reunion. Her brother's debts are remarkable – he has been barred from several London clubs – despite his title. As I have stated, his addiction to drinking and gambling grew hand-in-hand. I discovered that he did not visit his father often … in fact, he had not seen his father in years until he could no longer borrow any money on his own credit. Once home, he quarrelled with his half-sister, rather vehemently I have heard, but that is not the worst of it. His father, nearing death, asked his son to see to the care and future of his half-sister. He pleaded with his son to give up his sinful ways and to settle into the running of the estate and the title of earl … but, the son re-fused. He argued with his father in an alarming fashion, and … this is the part which I hesitate to say but it must be mentioned."

"I'm listening." The duke made an impatient gesture.

"It has been suggested that the viscount was responsible for his father's death," the older man uttered.

The duke raised an eyebrow. "Are you sug-gesting that John's son killed him?"

"I *am* suggesting it, but I am not alone in

this conjecture. The Earl of Chatham refused to give his son any money for drinking or cards. It is reported that his son flew into a terrible rage. Apparently, the servants report that it was that rage which brought about the death of the Earl of Chatman and the flight of his son."

He paused, as if he could not bear to announce more bad news. But still, he did. "There is also the matter of the threats to Lady Isabella."

"What sort of threats has he made?"

"She may not know of it, and I pray that she remains unaware of his vile words. Several of the servants overheard the viscount vowing that he would see his sister dead before she received one pound of her dowry or her annuity. If she does die unmarried, her dowry and her annuity become part of the property that will be inherited by her closest living male relative – in this case, her half-brother."

Matthew's eyebrows furrowed.

"I fear that such a depraved mind may contemplate further treachery and savagery. If he was willing to murder his father – a death, some say that was driven by the viscount's desperate need for money *and* for revenge."

Matthew was furious, but he hid it well. He was not normally a man who was prone to anger or any other emotion, and he would certainly not display any reaction in front of his subordinates or Mr Hayworth. Nevertheless, behind the veneer of civility and blandness that he wore on his face, he was filled with a dangerous kind of rage, an all-consuming one. John's son was implicated in his death, which was an act so abhorrent that he could scarcely comprehend it. Moreover, he was angered in equal measure by the threats made against Lady Isabella.

"What type of man seeks to destroy his own father and threatens his own half-sister?" The duke asked his question in a reserved fashion, one that concealed the underlying seething anger he felt.

"That question, Sir, is why the viscount is being sought by the local authorities. They are searching every port, every hamlet for any trace of him. He has been seen south of London, in the ports along the channel, but I do not know if he has fled the country. How dreadful to think that the viscount, a man who should be a paragon among his community, in fact, a fortunate young man who stands to inherit a vast estate and a noble title, could fall victim to depravity? The Earl of Chatham, God rest him, was the best of men, as you well know. He was respected, even revered by the people in his employ and under his care. Despite his propensity for travelling, he was well known and certainly well regarded in this country. His death, if it was the result of malicious intent, is not to be borne. Neither are the threats which may have prompted the earl to send his letter to you, the original missive which asked for your protection of his daughter."

"He knew me well enough to know that I would protect her against all threats, and that she would want for nothing in this world."

"Your character is well regarded, Sir. You

are as honourable an employer as one could wish for and a loyal friend if I may say so. But it is not my place to speak upon personal matters or presume to know more than I do."

Matthew gave an appreciative nod but did not smile. "I understand the need for your personal attention now, and the need for secrecy. I expect that you will continue to keep me abreast of all news regarding the viscount. Let me know when he has been apprehended and the outcome of the investigation, will you? In the meantime, it is imperative that Lady Isabella remains unaware of what we have discussed today. I do not wish for her to concern herself unduly with fears that have no substance while she is under my protection."

"I will see to it … *personally* … that you receive all news in complete confidence and at the highest expedience," the older man replied. "You have my word."

"You are a good man. You shall have a room to rest and refreshments will be sent to you at once. Your coachman and driver will be seen to as well. Stay as long as you need," the duke said as he rose from his chair, his jaw clenched tightly.

The man appeared relieved as he stood and bowed his head. "You are too kind. A cup of tea and a slice of bread would normally do me good, but I must confess a few hours' rest would be most welcome."

"You have earned it, Mr Hayworth. Cook will provide you any manner of drink and food you wish. My butler will see to it," Matthew replied, and he thought of Isabella Thornton. The woman who seemed to be so sure of herself, and who was so independent and clever, was in danger. He did not believe for a moment that she was the type of woman to show fear, to quake and quell with terror. Nor was she the kind to be weak-willed and tearful. But he did not wish to distress her any further. She had lost her father – she undoubtedly knew of her half-brother's weakness of character and of his animosity towards her. Their reported argument was evidence of that. If she could find solace and peace under his roof, he had no desire to jeopardise that, not for any amount of gold. It was the least he could do for John – and for her.

When Matthew thought of his old friend, he felt a dull ache of regret. Could he have done anything to save John's life from illness or the diabolical machinations of his own son? Matthew was a thinking man, clever, and educated. He knew that in truth, there was nothing he could have done to change what fate had ordained for his friend. Still, he vowed to do *all* that was in his vast and considerable power to protect John's daughter.

He thought of his friend, in his final hours, writing a letter filled with certainty that his old debt would be repaid. Matthew was determined that if he had to hunt for the scoundrel Charles Thornton, then he would make it his business to do so. Nothing would harm Isabella Thornton, nothing at all. He swore it upon his title and his family name.

CHAPTER 10

For the men and women who laboured ceaselessly to keep Hardwick Manor a grand residence and to ensure its reputation for good food, hospitality, and the best services afforded to the duke and his family, there were rules that had to be followed. Rules that everyone who called the gracious estate home had followed for countless generations. All the servants, from the highest-ranking butler and housekeeper, down to the lowest scullery maid and stable boy stayed in their realm, unless their duties required that they work among the family they served. This was how life had continued at Hardwick Manor since the first brick of it had been laid. But there was more to this small realm than slavish devotion. The division of duties and the unwritten rules and hierarchies of the servants' hall and grounds also functioned to ensure the smooth running of the whole, as everyone knew their place, their role and, to a great extent, their identity within the estate.

Isabella was only casually aware that her presence in the vegetable garden was generating a stir among the servants, who remained mostly silent as they observed her. She was wandering slowly among the cultivated rows in the vast garden to the south of the kitchen, the largest one of several carefully curated plots and by far the most important. In a house such as Hardwick Manor, vast amounts of food were required for the family and its servants. Autumn had arrived, and with it, the harvest. It was an exciting time of year for the gardeners as they reaped the fruits of the season's labours.

Isabella felt a little like a gardener herself, as she was beginning to feel almost hopeful about her prospects in London, and confident that the work that she and Diana had put into refining her ladylike skills was about to bear fruit.

She poked at this vegetable or that, examining the produce, and humming to herself as nearby, Mr Liddell, head gardener of the estate, stood and rubbed his eyes. He was an old, grizzled man whose face was tanned from too many summers spent in the sun, and whose hands were as gnarled as the crab apple trees that shaded the plot of soil he now stood upon. Valiantly, he tried to hide his pained expression but failed as he looked on, aghast. Isabella suspected he was asking himself, "What is she doing in my garden?"

Her intention was simple, and she would have replied, if he had asked her (which he dared not). She was bored. Since her afternoon ride with the duke, she had noticed a change in her life at the manor. The duke had forbidden her to ride, even accompanied, and she was no longer permitted to wander as she liked in the grounds. In fact, he had asked her to remain as much as possible in the company of his mother and sister. He had offered nothing in the way of an explanation for his request, other than to say he was certain the constant company of his female relatives would help prepare her for the London season. At the same time, more footmen had been engaged, and even now, she saw a sturdy fellow who seemed to have no particular purpose, lingering at the entrance to the kitchen garden. Surely, that had nothing to do with her?

MR LIDDELL HAD SEEN her father, the late Earl of Chatham, at the estate when the earl was a boy. Respect for the older man, and his title, made him hold his tongue as did his interest in remaining head gardener to the Duke of Devonshire. So, without much – if any – disagreement, he observed the beauty of the woman, with her lace-glove-covered hands, her expensive but sombre-coloured afternoon frock and her silk ribbon-lined straw bonnet, walking among the carefully maintained rows of his garden.

Isabella meandered from row to row, examining the plants until, at long last, she came to the end of a row of beans. "Mr Liddell, these look ready to harvest, shall I assist you?"

He could hardly say *no*. He and his lads were already working from sunup to sundown, to see that every piece of edible produce was harvested and stored for winter. What could not be stored, dried, or placed in the cold, dry cellars or high in the attics of the barns, was sent to Cook to preserve. He did not need any divertissement from his task, an important one that was vital to the sustenance of the estate. Not that the duke would balk at purchasing food during the winter, if he must. However, Mr Liddell would think such measures evidence of his own failure, and so he endured this visitor to his well-maintained green world, as he had numerous times before. In his judgement, the young woman who was poking about at his beans was nice enough for one of her sort, but she showed an odd interest in gardening and growing food – for a lady. If she were the daughter of a farmer, that would be one thing. He could understand that. But a high-born woman in his garden? That was nearly scandalous, wasn't it? Should she not be interested in prettier plants, such as flowers and rose buds, as his late mistress had been – not his beans – for Heaven's sake?

"My lady, I have boys to do the work, if you don't mind me saying so," he replied, clutching his hat in his hands, while wringing the brim.

"Oh, but your gardens are a credit to you, Mr Liddell. I have been all over the world, and these gardens are among the finest I have ever beheld. I lived for some time in Virginia, and the soil there is rich and fertile, but your garden shows truly astounding work. I commend you. You have coaxed so much from a lesser soil than we had in the colonies. If you would permit me, I would like to assist you in the harvest efforts." Her eyes twinkled as she smiled at a distant memory it seemed, although he also felt a small suspicion that she understood the dilemma she was causing him.

Mr Liddell did not know how to say *no*, but he said what he knew he had to. "Thank you, my lady, but please be careful not to soil your fancy dress. 'Tis hard work and not for the likes of one such as yourself, not when there are workers who can do the travail well enough."

"Mr Liddell, I will not mind a little bit of work – it will do me good," she replied, stripping away the lace gloves as she stood with her hands on her hips, looking as determined as any stubborn child.

Wiping his brow with a faded navy-blue handkerchief, he refrained from speaking his true thoughts as he nodded.

"I imagine you are correct, Miss."

. . .

ISABELLA WAS aware that this was not a real answer, in fact, it bordered as closely as the gardener could get to a negative reply. She knew that the servants found her presence in the garden odd, but she did not care at this moment. She was not offering to get behind the plough, for goodness sake – it was just a few beans! She was just about to begin on a row, when she noticed a familiar figure striding into view. The duke was dressed in his riding clothes and appeared as though he had just leapt down from his horse, which she presumed he had. His handsome face was flushed with exertion, and his hair was windblown in a way that only contributed to his good looks. For a moment, but just for a moment, the sight of him took her breath away. Mr Liddell, the old gardener, turned around and, as quickly as his old bones would allow, bowed before his master.

The duke acknowledged his head gardener with a nod and genuine smile, and then he laughed a deep and hearty laugh as he spotted

Isabella, their eyes meeting above the beans and tall plants.

"Lady Isabella?" he asked, his eyebrows raised in an expression of curiosity.

"Your Grace," she replied as she noted how well he appeared, even more so now that he was standing closer to her.

How long had it been since he stood within mere feet of her, his face turned to hers in a smile? He had been away attending to matters of business since the end of the summer season. She felt the stab of a sharp emotion she could not define and realised that she had missed his presence. It seemed that he had been engaged with other matters, even when he was in residence, as she had rarely seen him since that day of their ride together, several weeks earlier. Since noticing the changes in her freedoms at Hardwick Manor, there was much she wished to ask him about the restrictions now set upon her. However, she dared not ask, now that she had been discovered in his garden, like a disobedient child, and not the usual place for a proper young woman to be.

"What brings you to the garden?" he asked. "Did you tire of strolling along the terrace?"

"I did not tire of my daily strolls across the trees, but I found I wished for a larger area for my walks, and if I am not permitted to roam the grounds as I wish, then I thought I might make myself … useful … in other areas," she replied. She saw that Mr Liddell seemed as uncomfortable and awkward as she felt at that very moment. Looking down at her dress, she saw that her skirt had become tangled in the thick bean plant, and her shoes, a dainty pair of lady's boots had become quite dirty. She must surely be a sorry sight to the duke.

"You are the daughter of an earl, you have no need to make yourself *useful*," he remarked as he turned to his gardener. "Mr Liddell, I see that your efforts on behalf of the estate have proven to be exemplary with one exception. I wonder what manner of hazard has made its way into your beans?"

Mr Liddell stared at his master and then at her. Isabella could see that he was attempting not to smile. "The lady wants to help with the harvest, Sir."

"Does she?" the duke asked with the expression of a man who was teasing. "Come along out of the man's beans," his rebuke was softly, almost gently, given. "If you wish to be useful, you may provide *me* with a few minutes' distraction, as I return to the house by way of a walk."

Isabella could not decline his invitation. Nor did she want to. Careful not to injure the bean plants, she tried to unwind the long green tendrils from her skirt. The duke stepped forward, between the rows and held out his hand, as a plain offer to help her rise from her near-crouched position. Isabella, whose hands were still bare, reached out to accept. She noticed then, that he was not wearing his riding gloves. Despite the oddness of their situation, she felt her heart skip a beat at the touch of his skin on her hand. It was smooth and cool, but not as soft as one might expect of someone who had not been born to a life of manual work. Rather his hands were firm and solid, similar – she imagined – to their owner. She was sure that she had reddened at the thoughts that his touch evoked, and she stood quickly. The duke's supporting hand held her steady, and he released her as soon as she stepped out of the garden.

Impulsively, she slid her gloves back on and then touched her bonnet and hair. Was it in place? Had any of her dark curls escaped?

She tried not to make herself any more wretched and out of place than she must already appear. Isabella could not help but notice the look of relief on Mr Liddell's face. *The poor man,* she thought. How inconsiderate she had been in her thoughtless boredom. She had not wished to add to his hardships.

"Mr Liddell, I am sorry to have troubled you," she said to the older man who looked at her with a wide-eyed expression that she presumed indicated some kind of astonishment.

"You haven't troubled me, my lady," he said,

but she had a feeling that the gardener was simply too polite or too aware of his master, standing not more than a few feet away.

"You are too kind, Mr Liddell," she replied as she felt the gaze of the duke fall upon her face. He was staring at her, there was no doubt about it. For a moment, she wondered if he recognised the need she had to move and do something, anything. It was that need that had pushed her to make her ridiculous offer to help with the beans.

"Walk with me, Lady Isabella," the duke said.

He turned in the direction of the flower garden, or what was left of it in September. The blooms of summer had long since disappeared, and the trees were shedding orange-and-gold leaves in the cool breeze of early autumn. Isabella enjoyed walking. It was one of her favourite activities, but today, she felt strangely anxious.

As they walked side by side, the duke seemed to take his time before he spoke. "You continue to astonish me. I am away for weeks, and when I return to my estate, I find you among the vegetables."

"I will not apologize for my interest in growing things. And the garden lies so close to the house. I am grateful for your care of me, and I hope I did not cause Mr Liddell too much distress. I do understand that the garden is no place for a lady to offer her help. I do not know what came over me." She did know, she recognised her own growing alarm and sense of being confined by the duke's request to stay close to his mother and sister.

"If you know this, then I can only guess that you have distressed my gardener for sport," he said, but his words were softened by the hint of amusement in his voice.

"Please, Your Grace, of course not! I beg you not to make me feel any more foolish than I already do. What could I have been thinking? Did you see how he looked at me? It was as though I was an invader, and his garden was England itself."

"Mr Liddell will survive any wound you

may have caused" – a smile formed on his lips – "a slight at the most, I assure you. If it brings you comfort, I can faithfully report that he has always shown a peculiar territoriality when it comes to those plots of earth that are under his charge."

"It is true that your gardens are among the finest I have seen," she said.

"A feat for which I cannot take any credit. That would be entirely Mr Liddell's doing … and his forefathers, all of whom have served our family. Good Heavens, how many years has it been?" the duke said, his lips curved.

"I suppose Mr Liddell feels as though the estate is as much his as it is yours. No wonder he was distraught when I was standing in his beans." She giggled.

"Tell me – why were you in the garden?"

"You will think me ungrateful."

"I give you my word that I will not. Well, I will try my best, at the very least," he responded without a hint that he was teasing her.

"Very well. I do not feel that I have wronged

anyone … not truly. Although Mr Liddell did seem vaguely concerned that I might trample his plants at any moment like a wild donkey." She laughed. "Oh, the poor man. But, you wished to know why I was drawn to the gardens? I shall tell you, but I do not think you will find the answer very interesting."

He nodded in curiosity and gestured for her to carry on.

"I developed an interest in such things during my travels with my father. I did not become aware of how strange my interest in gardening was, as a woman, until I came home to England. When we travelled, we often stayed in houses that boasted enormous gardens and contained all manner of plants. I have seen fruits and vegetables of incredible variety in the warmer climates, some quite large and colourful. I even grew my own garden when we lived in Virginia! It was illuminating! I adored the hours I spent cultivating food and flowers. There is a lot to be said for seeing something larger spring from some small hours of toil."

She laughed a little. "I realise that sounds suspiciously as if I am yearning for the life of a common labourer."

"I wonder, is it merely a wish for a simpler life?" His voice sounded genuinely interested. "Having said that," he paused reflectively, "we English almost venerate men such as Capability Brown, and I freely admit I considered his landscape designs myself, when changing parts of the estate's layout."

Isabella nodded, grateful that he had not dismissed her thoughts. "It is just a wish to make things grow – a pastime I once derived great pleasure from when I was younger and when I was permitted to do as I wished." She was careful not to hint at her feelings of rest-lessness.

"Are you speaking in earnest? You would work in a garden? You are a wealthy young woman of privilege, who has no need to ever lift a tool or plant a single seed."

"I find time spent in the garden to be like riding. It can be exhilarating at times and sometimes rather peaceful. I find the pursuit most inspirational and joyous. Riding allows a person to free themselves, both physically and mentally, and gardening can bring that same liberation to the spirit."

The duke stopped walking and stared at her in a way that she could not fathom. "You are unlike any woman I have ever met. Proper ladies do not go about in vegetable gardens or care to dirty their hands in any pursuit."

"Then I must conclude that I am not a proper lady," she said.

"I have seen you as a proper lady and as yourself." The duke's gaze was on her. "You most certainly do not always behave as convention dictates you should. Understand that is not said to cause offense. There are times when I find proper ladies to be as predictable as the seasons."

"I suppose I have my father to thank for my unconventional ways. He encouraged me to act and say as I wished. He was a remarkable man."

"He *was* remarkable – from the first time I

met him. I remember it well. I do not know if he told you the tale of our meeting, but it was a thrilling one."

Isabella shook her head.

"I was making a rather misguided attempt to save a puppy, belonging to my late wife. Of course, we were not married then. I was but a child and so was she. Your father was the one who saved my life – and that of the dog, I might add – but it was me who received Georgiana's gratitude. If I am not greatly mistaken, I owe your father an even larger debt than I realised, back then. She often said that she married me because of my heroics that day."

Isabella was nearly stunned. It was the first time that she could recall that the Duke of Devonshire had ever spoken of either her father – or his dead wife. For that matter, she could not recall such a pleasant conversation with him. She was short of words, and so she said nothing, but waited for him to continue.

"When I think of you in the garden, ignoring the rules of polite society, I am reminded of how independent Georgiana was in her day. Do not mistake me, she was a true lady … as a duchess she could not have been anything else. But she did possess her own opinions and her own way of doing things. If she had been the one to find you in the garden, I think she may have joined you in your efforts – at least until she could have convinced you to come inside for a nice cup of tea."

"I should have liked to have met her," said Isabella warmly.

"She was taken away from me, from Hardwick Manor, far too soon."

A question formed in her mind and she almost did not dare to ask.

"How did she die?" she asked softly. "If you do not mind my asking."

"She died in a carriage accident, not far from the estate," he said, and his voice remained strong, but his eyes betrayed a deeply lingering sadness.

"That must have been dreadful," Isabella replied quietly, suddenly aware of the chirping of the birds in the trees overhead as the chilly breeze became a colder wind that stirred the branches.

"I don't know who mourned her more, me or my mother," the duke continued. "My mother doted on Georgiana, and Diana was inconsolable. She was so young, and she thought of Georgiana as an older sister. She idolised her, everyone did."

"How terrible for you and your family. I am sorry for your loss, Sir." She gave him a kind glance. She wanted to touch his shoulder, but then she decided against it. He looked into her eyes, and for a moment, they both paused.

"I have been careless ..." The duke trailed off and broke the silence. "I have spoken of my loss when yours is still fresh. Your father was a dear friend. I respected him and held him in the highest regard. Yet, when I was first married – and *during* my marriage also, if I am honest – I was consumed by my good fortune, and I drifted apart from your father. After the death of my wife, I felt myself more alone than

I had ever imagined possible, and this made me unable to nourish my friendships, not only to him, but to other friends equally. Forgive me ... I have been selfish, thinking of my own grief when yours is yet a few months old."

Isabella was touched by his sentiment.

"I appreciate your saying this, when it is obviously so deeply painful for you to recount it. I venture to guess that I am well-placed to know at least a part of the pain you felt at losing your companion so suddenly. That is how I felt when my father took ill so quickly, and I finally understood that our adventures were at an end, and that I would lose the only person who truly loved me. His loss *was* terrible. I have missed him every day, it seems. If I may speak candidly, I am rather envious of you."

"Envious?"

"Yes, I am envious of you, Sir. You had your sister and your mother around you, who shared your loss and the love you had for your wife. When my father died, I had no one close to me to share the burden of his passing. My mother had been dead for many years and … my half-brother is not fond of me. His last words to me were said in anger." She looked into his eyes. "If it was not for your family, I should have felt very alone indeed. I am incredibly grateful to you for allowing me to stay here. Your mother and sister have been more than kind to me."

Isabella felt his gaze upon her. It was thoughtful and silent as though it was quietly reproachful. Gone were his smile and the teasing manner that he had displayed so enthusiastically when he first came across her in the garden. Had she spoken too frankly? Had she been too honest in the giving of her opinions on the matters of loss and tragedy?

He continued to study her before saying, rather abruptly, "We should return to the house. The weather is changing. I have no wish to see you made ill by it."

She was reminded of their summer ride along the dales. That precious moment that they shared when they had been happy in each other's company, smiling and laughing as they enjoyed the lush green landscape, as they found something that they shared in common. He had seemed cheerful that summer's day, which seemed so long ago. Then, too, just as quickly, he had turned and become distant towards her, as if he had no wish to speak to her.

She studied him as he silently escorted her back to his house. How could he be so charming in one moment and then so disagreeable in the next? Were her actions, her behaviour so dreadful that she was unable to earn his respect or his regard? No, she decided. There must be a reason behind his actions, one she could, and needed not know.

Striding with purpose up the stone steps that led to the house, she recalled the myriad of questions she still wished to ask him. About the sentries and the footmen, and his travels which seemed to keep him away. However, she was unable to ask him a single question as he took his leave of her as soon as they were inside the house. She watched as he strode away, undoubtedly heading for his study, and she heard the heavy wooden door of his sanctuary close with a definite clang. Had she angered him in some way? She did not know the answer to that question, and would probably never find out. Not when she knew he would always be an enigma, a quiet man who would remain alone and mysterious for the rest of his life.

CHAPTER 11

*A*utumn had arrived completely at Hardwick Manor, with the brilliant fanfare of colour that heralded the coming cold weather of winter.

Mr Liddell had overseen the harvest of the kitchen gardens in his usual efficient manner, his lads working non-stop as they plucked, picked, and dug everything edible that would see the manor through the long cold winter. With Mr Liddell's work now done, Isabella noted how he had turned his attention to preparing the stately ornamental gardens and arbours for the cold, but it appeared as though his work was not as pressing, and the walled pleasure gardens assumed an air of tranquillity after so much fervent activity and seemed to breathe a collective sigh of exhausted contentment.

That serenity, like a blissful rest after a long and arduous journey, was a much-needed panacea to Isabella. Walking along the garden paths, she absorbed the last of the warm rays of sunshine among the golden leaves, the reds and crimsons, and the deep burgundies of the majestic oaks, the enormous beech and alders shading her way. The wind rustled in the branches overhead, and a light breeze blew among the swirling leaves as they landed softly in front of her feet, crunching under her soft shoes. In a season such as this, in the gardens of Hardwick Manor, she could permit herself to breathe in the cool air, and to savour the scent of the woodsmoke that curled up from the kitchen chimney nearby.

It was on such an afternoon, when Isabella

remained out until sunset, that she was able to imagine that her life would always be this way: leaves swirling around her, the slight tingling of the cold on her cheeks. In the quiet of the garden, she could imagine that nothing bad had ever happened to her, and that she was free to marry whomever she chose – that she was the daughter of an earl with a thousand prospects laid out before her. She could almost forget the duke, his changeable nature, and the debt that she owed him. Closing her eyes, she tried not to think about the rare moments when he smiled and laughed, and the more common instances when he did not. It was on these occasions that she could also imagine that her half-brother had not sworn to hate her.

She walked through the arbour, in the last of the sunlight of that autumn afternoon, savouring the purples and indigo shadows that fell as the sun set behind the horizon into a gathering gloom that she found surprisingly comforting. She emerged from the dark tunnel of the arbour, her face turned towards the house. Candlelight already glowed in the windows, and she imagined that Lady Diana and her mother would be spending the better part of two hours having their hair curled, while she was latching onto a few minutes of welcome quiet like a mischievous child. She found it helped to ease her sorrow, more than any music lesson or new dress could. Although, she had to admit, that on this afternoon, she had spent more time thinking about the duke than she would have wished. He was still an enigma to her, and she decided that he always would be.

Occupied as her thoughts were by the duke, she moved carelessly, as though she was in no danger inside the walled garden of the estate. With her head back, and her eyes firmly fixed on the house in front of her, she walked steadily and purposely. Suddenly however, she realised that she was not alone in the garden.

She caught a shadow, a sudden movement, out of the corner of her eye, and she stopped. Staring in the direction of one of the numerous wooden doors that were built into the garden walls, she willed herself to see past the shadows and the gloom to what could have caused her alarm. She was not sure whether she believed in ghosts and other beings of the supernatural world, but they must surely be out – she had been told that this was their special time in stories from her youth. She had not believed such tales to be true, and dismissed them as tales told to thrill the servants and the common people, but now, as she stood still in the last light of the day, she began to wonder if her confidence in her own certainty might be falsely placed.

After a few minutes, Isabella decided that she was being foolish. How had she arrived at such an unreasonable interpretation, that a darting shadow or a glint of light heralded a denizen from the other world? *What a perfectly ridiculous conclusion,* she thought to herself. She was probably seeing nothing more than a servant rushing along the path to some unknown destination, or a late season bird rustling in the bushes. When nothing else happened to trouble her, she became certain that she was not in any danger of encountering a spectral ancestor of the duke – or, for that matter, her half-brother.

What she had seen must have been a servant – it could not have been anybody else. Yes, she grew more convinced of her error, as she walked towards the house, crossing a wide expanse of lawn. However, her shaky confidence was quickly dashed, and she was overtaken by fear once more, when she thought she saw something glide past her, just out of her direct line of vision. Turning abruptly, a laugh escaped her. The sound of her voice was high and melodic in the cool air.

Entwined in the nearby bushes was a length of ribbon. It was light blue and nearly incandescent against the leaves that held it in place. It reminded her of the hue that Lady Diana favoured. Still, she could not understand why a length of expensive ribbon should be here in the garden, when Lady Diana was undoubtedly inside the house, her maid earnestly styling her hair into the latest fashion. Reaching for the ribbon with her gloved hand, Isabella noted that it was carefully cut on the ends, as if purposely trimmed. It surely must have been lost while Diana (or some other lady) was in the garden, and the wind had carried it here for her to find. She laughed again. How silly she had been to permit herself to be fearful of shadows in the waning light.

Was she so foolish to fear the gloom? Her half-brother might be lurking, after all. It was a terrible, dreadful thought, but one that she was quick to entertain. No one had spoken to her about him, nor had she wished to discuss him with her protectors. There could be no doubt that he might wish to see her. If for no other reason than to frighten her or to seek revenge.

She shivered as she grasped the ribbon more tightly, intending to take it into the house with her. Then she heard a creaking sound. It jolted her from her reverie and examination of the ribbon. She thought she detected movement towards the wall, in the same place as before. She was positive that she glimpsed a hint of crimson among the branches and leaves that was not part of the foliage. For only a second, and no more, she was forced to accept her previous alarming idea that she was not alone in the enormity of the garden. She shuddered. The wind rose around her, and suddenly the ribbon was snatched from her fingers. She watched it take flight, as if plucked by unseen and unnatural hands. As she followed its progress into the darkness, she tried not to think about the sound she recognised, as day turned to evening: the unmistakable, soft tread of footsteps growing fainter as they moved off into the distance.

IN THE DAYS that followed that evening, Isabella did not venture into the garden at all. She was helped by a turn in the weather, as a cold wind announced that winter was hastening quickly on autumn's heels.

On a particularly pleasant day, after the

winds had vanished, Isabella had ridden out with a groom in the afternoon, and was glad to have rediscovered that she felt comfortable and happy on the manor's grounds, which by day were friendly and full of autumn's colours.

They had dined companionably that evening, and now she had escaped the warmth of the dining room to stand for a while on the balcony in the crisp evening air. A harvest moon hung limply in the dark-blue sky, hugging the horizon as if it, too, were reluctant to admit that winter was coming. A faint scent of the cut stalks of the harvest grain carried to her on the breeze.

In their beds, small lavender-coloured asters had come alive in the rapidly fading autumn light, and appeared like stars that had fallen from the sky. With a cashmere shawl around her shoulders, Isabella felt warm and content.

She wondered what it would be like to be the lady of such a manor, and to be a part of the manor's yearly cycle – of growth and harvest, and of the local life and parties from the city. As if in answer to her thoughts, she heard the door to the dining room open and smelled the scent of cigar smoke that told her the manor's real owner had joined her on the balcony. She stood motionless for a moment, attempting not to flush at the mere image of her musings.

"Lady Isabella." He acknowledged her presence, even though they had dined together half an hour before.

"Your Grace." She smiled, and he crossed to stand beside her at the balcony's balustrade.

"A beautiful sight," he said.

Isabella continued to look out across the flower beds, but from the corner of her eye, it appeared to her that he was staring at her as he spoke. She reddened, but the falling light hid the ever-brightening colour of her cheeks.

"It is," she replied. "You are extremely fortunate indeed, Sir, to have such a wonderful home. I am incredibly grateful that you have allowed me to share it, if only for a limited time."

He seemed to start a bit at her comment and said, "I hope you are not planning on leaving us too soon, Lady Isabella." He seemed to consider his words for a moment, before adding, "Or, does the gardening world call you from us to another harvest?" He smiled then, undoubtedly to soften his words so she understood his plainly intended humour.

She laughed, and, seemingly encouraged, he stepped closer to her to add, "Having witnessed your talents first-hand, I could not deny them to another gardener somewhere in our county."

"You mock me, Sir." She pretended offence, but her smile gave way to the falsity of her words.

"Then, please accept my apology," he said gently, "although I am sure you are not the type of woman who takes offence easily, especially where none is intended."

"No, Sir," she assured him. "I have a sense of humour, even when it concerns myself. In truth, my response was that which is expected of a refined lady rather than the feelings of this particular lady."

He seemed unsure of how to respond, and she added, "Surely, you agree, I must take every opportunity to use the excellent and kind advice I receive from your mother and sister about how a woman of society should act and speak in the presence of a gentleman." She smiled to reveal there was no malice in her words.

"If that means you cannot speak as freely as you would wish, then I hope you do not absorb too much of their teachings, Lady Isabella. Although" — he paused — "to the best of *my* knowledge, neither my mother nor sister have ever refrained from expressing their completely frank opinions. Certainly not to me."

At this they both began to laugh, and Isabella realised that there was a softness and humour to this man that she had not seen before.

They had each turned towards each other during this exchange, and now they were staring directly into one another's eyes. Isabella again noticed the mesmerising dark-brown depth in his gaze. In the moonlight, they seemed to sparkle. Another emotion also lay within, a warmer, more serious one, and Isabella felt a response rising within her being.

Was he leaning closer?

He was! *Much* closer, in fact.

His voice was unexpectedly soft. "Lady Isabella, I want to—"

What he wanted was suddenly lost to them both, as the snick of the dining room door announced the arrival of the dowager duchess. The duke abruptly stopped speaking, and Isabella turned her gaze towards the duchess.

The duchess cleared her throat quite loudly. "I do hope I have not interrupted a serious topic of conversation."

Isabella could not utter a word.

"Not at all, Mother," the duke replied smoothly. "We were only enjoying the cool evening."

"Come inside, children. It has become *too* cold to stand out here chatting!" she called to them. Isabella was certain the dowager duchess had not chosen her form of address deliberately – but she still reminded the duke of his duty to his family and Isabella of her role as his ward.

As they obeyed and crossed the expanse of the balcony, Isabella wondered what he had been about to say – or do. She had felt a rush of blood to her cheeks as she lifted her eyes to him, and she was certain she had seen her emotions reflected in his face. Would he have intended to … kiss her, had his mother remained inside? No, that was ridiculous. Or was it not? She did not know if her suspicions were correct. She could not be completely certain, but for the briefest of moments, she thought she saw a flash of emotion cross the duke's dark gaze. Dare she hope?

CHAPTER 12

It was early January. Snow fell outside the tall windows of the drawing room, which was the showcase of the stately mansion overlooking Hyde Park in London. With its damask-covered walls, marble mantel piece and its rich furnishings, it was meant to impress any visitor who was fortunate enough to be invited into this splendid room. However, the priceless rugs, the silk pillows, the floral-upholstered tufted chairs, and the paintings that were arranged to display their grandeur to its best benefit, all went unnoticed by Isabella Thornton. She only had eyes for the grey clouds that dumped white flakes onto the white-covered ground outside. Winter was beautiful. She was lost in her own thoughts as she looked out the window listlessly, leaning against the window frame watching her breath as it steamed up the glass.

Her figure was adorned in a blue-striped afternoon dress, her dark-brown hair curled and caught with a fashionable blue ribbon. Isabella was no longer in mourning. Her new clothes – in addition to any of her old ones that could be salvaged from her months of mourning – were mixed and matched in accordance with Diana and the duchess's instructions as to what was fashionable.

She had accompanied Diana, the dowager duchess, and the duke to London. Autumn, like summer, was as distant to her as a fleeting dream. However, Isabella had cause for some happiness as she remarked that the warmth of summer lingered in the subtle changes she saw and felt in the duke's demeanour towards her.

True, he was often away and busy, even when he was in town, and yet she felt his warm regard in small gestures and looks. While in residence in London, he was often absent from the drawing room, and, except by necessity, at dinner or when there were guests – which was not often as it was still quite early in the social season. Despite this, he had sought her out on occasion, just to enquire after her well-being. Those small moments kept returning to her in the evenings as she lay waiting for sleep, and she often drifted off with a smile on her lips.

Diana was chirping happily about the social season from the fireside, and she entreated Isabella to join her.

"Do come away from the window," Diana said, "there is nothing to see outside except snow and more snow. All it does is snow these days. How I long for spring once more, with the flowers in bloom and the birds in the trees."

"My dear, that is not what is important, not when we have much to discuss," the duchess began.

There was no escaping the inevitability of Isabella and Diana's presentation. Diana was excited, that came as no surprise. Her enthusiasm for the event (which was scheduled to occur in a week) was nearly as infectious as her smile. Even the dowager duchess was affected by her daughter's exuberance. The older woman beamed at her daughter with pride, and to nearly the same extent at her charge, Lady Isabella. Or so it seemed to Isabella who noted the way the duchess looked at her, not aghast, but with a warm regard that endeared her to Isabella even more.

These past few months had been a whirlwind of Christmas festivities – planning for the season, ordering dresses, and finally, when she was established as a young heiress who was to be correctly introduced into society. In addition to the bewildering choices of bonnets and gloves, and of being fitted for her new wardrobe, the duchess had compelled Isabella to submit to some hastily arranged, last-minute tutoring in all manner of subjects from music to drawing. In all of these activities, Isabella had been far too busy to think about the duke and his absence.

"My dear, you do not look at all as I would presume a young lady should who is about to be presented," the Duchess of Devonshire said to Isabella, as she sat down beside Diana. "Sit by the fire and warm yourself. You have spent far too much time by the window ... I wonder, have you caught a chill? You are rather pale."

Diana had been busy with embroidery, but now she ignored her hoop and thread to look up. She stared at Isabella with unmasked concern on her features. "She *does* look pale. We cannot have our dear Lady Isabella ill – not when she is about to become the belle of London society!"

"I assure you that I am not ill." Isabella tried to placate the two women.

"That would never do," the duchess declared. "Lady Isabella, draw near to the fire. I do say you have taken a chill. Standing by the windows without a shawl on your shoulders is not advisable during such inclement weather as this. I cannot recall seeing so much snow in one season before this year. We shall all be fortunate that we do not suffer from influenza before the spring. I shall instruct the butler to tell Cook to prepare broth for everyone. Diana, do you think we should send for the doctor?"

"No, please do not trouble the doctor ... I do not feel in any way feverish," Isabella said as brightly as she could manage. "I did not mean to alarm either of you. If you would continue to discuss the plans for the ball, I am looking forward to it with great interest."

The duchess was not easily deceived. She leaned in close to Isabella. "If you insist that you are well, I shall take you at your word. Still, I have you under my eye. If I detect the slightest flush, the least indication that you are unwell, I shall send for Dr Gordon, and that shall be an end to it."

"I am well, I give you my vow. If I am pale, it is from the thrill of the upcoming season."

"Are you sure? I fear it may be more than

that. You cannot deceive me. What troubles you, my dear?" The duchess was adamant.

"You can tell us. You can tell us *anything* you like," Lady Diana replied with a reassuring nod.

"I do not want to trouble anyone. You have all been so dear to me. You took me in and cared for me as I had no right to expect."

"We would not have wanted it any other way," Diana said firmly.

"It is nothing, my dear, nothing at all. Your father was a darling boy who I had the privilege to see grow into manhood," the older woman agreed. "I regret that I did not see more of him after he became the earl, but that is regret and age speaking. You are as welcome to stay with me as though you were my own niece. You have not troubled us in the slightest."

Isabella was moved by their generous spirits. "I could not have asked for a better reception than the one I have received from both of you. It is for that very reason that I hesitate to mention any cause for worry or concern. This is a happy time."

"I could not agree more. Both you and I are about to become the most eligible young women in all of London." Diana could not help but interject affectionately, as she so often did. "I dare say, I will be married soon." She smiled at Isabella. "But I should not be the only one of us who is to be married. With your beauty and your cleverness, I do not think any gentleman shall wish to miss an opportunity to dance and dine with you."

Isabella was relieved that the mood of the drawing room had once again returned to its happy state, but she was not to be permitted to let it remain so. The duchess was unrelenting. "Tell us what worries you. If we can be of help, we shall."

"If you insist." Isabella sighed, her shoulders slumping as she exhaled, her lips set in a frown. "I fear I have been far too troublesome to His Grace, but that is another matter. What concerns me, and I hesitate to speak of it, is my half-brother and ... my dowry. These two subjects are tied together, tied I fear without hope of resolution."

"Your half-brother?" The duchess raised her eyebrows.

"You do not speak of him, so we have not enquired," Lady Diana said.

"No, I do not speak of him. My memories of him, and what transpired between us, are far too painful. He and I were never close – not in the way that you are with your brother, His Grace," Isabella explained. "What is worse is that I fear that because the matter of his succession to my father's title and inheritance is unsettled, I am not certain of my dowry or much else. It is all rather confusing and, I fear, unfortunately, unresolved. My solicitor has been forced to wait while my half-brother is located. I do not know why he has disappeared, but he has – and with him, all hopes of resolving my future."

Lady Diana's quizzical expression became a deep-set look of confusion as she glanced from

Isabella to the duchess, as if she were searching for answers.

"How dreadful! Do you not know whether you shall receive your dowry? What will be your rank if we are to introduce you to someone?"

"It is dreadful, and a matter I had hoped would be brought to a swift conclusion in the summer … however, it has lingered on past all hope of ever being settled. My father's title is not yet entailed. His estate hangs in uncertainty, and my dowry is not yet untouched. But, I do not wish to trouble either of you with my concerns – not when there is to be a ball and gaiety and merriment."

The duchess made a harrumphing sound. "*You* should not worry yourself about such things. My dear, you are far too young and have been through entirely too much tragedy to trouble yourself with matters of money and inheritance. Your solicitors should have spoken for you. It was their duty to get this situation well in hand. But has your half-brother truly disappeared?"

"He vanished very shortly after my father's death." Isabella nodded. "I have not seen nor spoken to him since. It is a sad thing to aver, but I do not miss him because he was rather vehement in the expression of his ... *dislike* of me when we last met. In truth, now that we are in London, I fear that I may see him again."

"How so?" The duchess and Diana seemed to hang on her every word.

"While I was at Hardwick Manor, I felt safer from him and his cruel disregard. In the country, he could not reach me easily, or so I told myself. But here, in London, where I know he resided before our father's death, I dread that he will seek me out and do all he can to make me miserable. Truth be known, aside from the inconvenience of not having my dowry settled, I would prefer not to be regarded as Charles's half-sister at all. I should not be saying this, but it was told to me by my maid, a woman whom you both know I trust far more than a servant. She confided in me that my half-brother owed a great deal of money because of gaming and" – she swallowed – "excessive drinking. It is an embarrassment and a reputation that I do not wish to share."

"Lady Isabella, how have you kept this horrid secret from us?" Lady Diana exclaimed. "How resolute you must be, and how *strong*. How have you remained so agreeable? I could never have hidden such strong emotions and feelings, not even for a *minute*. I would have wept every second of every day if I were faced with such adversity."

"Diana, not every woman is as carefree and well looked after as you are, my dear. Do not embarrass our Lady Isabella with such foolish opinions," chided the Duchess of Devonshire.

Lady Diana did not seem to suffer the criticism for long. She shook off any humiliation and continued in her joyful way. "I should not have mentioned anything about it. Shall we discuss something far merrier to take our minds off such a dark topic? Shall we discuss the musicians who are playing for the ball? I have heard that they come highly recommended and are skilled at the most popular country dances!" Lady Diana clapped her hands and widened her eyes. "Oh, my dear Lady Isabella, I have nearly forgotten Lady Bentinck's introduction of what many ladies in society believe to be a most scandalous dance! She will be hosting a ball, as well. It is a foreign waltz where couples dance closely together – the entire time!"

Isabella was grateful for the resumption of a more joyous topic of conversation and she added her opinion of the latest dances, all of which she had learned from her dance tutor at Hardwick Manor. She permitted her own troubles to be pushed aside, and she did not think it unusual when the duchess excused herself from the drawing room, with the excuse of seeing about a change in the dinner menu.

· · ·

THE DUCHESS HAD NOT BEEN truthful. She did not walk downstairs to see Cook, but instead, upon exiting the drawing room, chose to march straight to her son's study, as a general going to war. The revelation of Lady Isabella's state of affairs was most dire and needed to be handled swiftly. The duchess was unyielding, and she would not rest until there was a solution as to how she could help this young woman.

THE DUKE'S polished oak desk was covered in leather-bound books, and ledgers that included details about mortgages and payments from tenants. He felt it a rather tedious business which consumed far too much of his time for his liking, and he would rather have been riding in Hyde Park even upon a day as snowy and inhospitable as this one. Despite having a trusted staff of agents and appointed men to see to things such as managing his tenants and his properties (which were vast), he oversaw a large amount of the bookkeeping himself. Ultimately, he made it a habit – a habit that was ingrained in him from a young age – to review the final accounts personally. He was just finishing a row of numbers of rent paid and mortgages that were current, when he rubbed his eyes and looked up. His mother, who did not ordinarily come to see him while he was working, stood in the doorway. She knocked and entered with a determined look on her face. At first sight, he welcomed the distraction that his mother's visit to the study must surely herald, but her resolute features foretold that this visit did not concern the ball or any details of the coming festivities. He knew that she had something far more serious to warrant such a stern expression – *and* the interruption.

Closing an account book, he slid the volume and its companions into a stack, making sure to remember the column and the page he had just been studying. When he invited his mother to sit, he felt worried.

"You appear troubled, Mother. Please be seated, and tell me – what concerns you?"

She did as he asked. Her face retained its near scowl as she began, "You are aware that since the death of your father, I have done little to interfere in the managing of the estates or the responsibilities of your position. I have rarely offered my opinion or judgement. Today, I must speak to you regarding a sensitive matter, which I fear is most urgent."

Matthew felt a surge of relief, thinking that the matter of which she spoke concerned the upcoming event to be held in his mansion and not, as he had feared, her worry about his marital status. "Urgent? Mother, is there some reason I should be concerned? Does this pertain to the ball?"

"No, no, son. It does not. Would I have bothered you with concerns as trivial as the ball? I have been planning such events with great success for many years. I do not need your opinion on such subjects. No, Matthew, this concerns something far more delicate and more important. I have come to you on behalf of Lady Isabella."

He was suddenly animated. "Lady Isabella?"

The sudden change in his demeanour was observed by his mother, but, thankfully, she did not speak about it, as she continued, "She is well, but I fear she may fall ill from an attack of nerves if nothing is done to relieve her troubles. This afternoon, when she should have been worried about her gown fitting or the dances she should learn, she confessed that she has concerns about her brother and her dowry. I ask you, why should a woman of her tender age be concerned with anything more pressing than her presentation at court and her coming-out ball? Did you know that she is afraid of her half-brother? Lady Isabella has had the graciousness not to state it exactly, but she speaks of him with such dread. Then there is the matter of her dowry. Her solicitors have written to tell her that the estate of her father remains unsettled. How is she to be wed, if her dowry is not settled upon her?"

"I know that you and Lady Isabella have grown close," Matthew replied, "but I did not think that you would concern yourself regarding her dowry or her half-brother."

"Why would I not concern myself with her? She has lived with us for some time, and I have come to regard her as family, even if she is not related to us by blood." The duchess was defiant. "I presume you feel equally responsible for her. Although, I do wonder that you have spent a considerable amount of time away the last few weeks. In light of what I have discovered from her, that she is fearful of her half-brother, I wonder if your being away was in her best interests?"

"I have not spoken about her dowry or her half-brother to you, Diana, or Lady Isabella for the sole reason that I did not wish to cause any one of you distress or cause for alarm. I may seem rather callous, or unaware of the circumstances, but I give you my word that I am far more aware of matters regarding Lady Isabella than her own solicitors."

The duchess raised her eyebrows as he continued.

"There is no need to be troubled. I shall stand for her dowry, if she has none, and I shall see that she is protected from her half-brother. Is there anything else which has given you cause for doubt or worry?"

"Do not expect to dismiss me so quickly," his mother replied.

"I will do my duty to her father. No harm shall come to her. She is my responsibility, and I intend to see that she is well cared for" – He paused for a moment – "until such time as a gentleman can be found as a husband."

"I would like to know what measures you have taken, and how have these concerns been resolved? I, myself, have *just* become aware of them. Are you admitting that you have known of Lady Isabella's troubles for some time? How so? Did she tell you?"

Matthew shook his head. "She has not spoken to me of any of the worries she may have expressed to you. Still, that does not mean that I was ignorant of them. I asked Mr Hayworth to ascertain her circumstances, and he did his job with his usual diligence and skill. I was made aware of the troubling history between Lady Isabella and her half-brother – and of other matters which I do not wish to speak of, just yet. As to her protection, I have seen to it that she was never in any danger. Have you not noticed the additional men I have hired at Hardwick Manor, the restrictions I have placed upon Lady Isabella's riding and walks, or the cause of my travels?"

"I wondered, but then I did not think anything of it, until now. Please continue, son."

"In confidence, I tell you that her half-brother *must* be found, at all costs. There are questions which he must answer, and charges he must face. Moreover, I have spent a considerable amount of time aiding in the search for the man and hiring men to try to locate him."

"Oh, my goodness – and what has come of this?"

"I have been told that he shall soon be in custody."

The duchess appeared astonished. "Custody? I do wish you would speak plainly. I am not likely to faint, nor am I going to tell Lady Isabella anything that is said in confidence. Continue, son, continue."

"Her brother is wanted for questioning about the murder of their father."

The duchess's eyes grew huge.

"That is the reason her father's estate and inheritance are unsettled. That is the cause for the additional men at Hardwick Manor and for my travels. And that is why I did not mention it, either, because I did not wish to cause Lady Isabella any further anguish. I will not rest until he is found, and she is safe. The dowry is of minor importance. For John's sake and for hers, I shall provide every pound of it, if I must."

THE DOWAGER DUCHESS wanted to smile, but she dared not. It was like playing cards. She had no desire to show her son her hand, or in this case, that she knew what cards he may be holding. Her son had been secretly protecting Lady Isabella, searching all of England – it would seem – for her half-brother.

In her experience, this could only mean one thing. The duchess took a long look at her son. Then she was certain. She realised that her son harboured feelings for Lady Isabella, feelings that he had yet to admit, even to himself. As she concealed her happy astonishment from her son, she had no way of knowing (and neither did he) that more than just the duchess's joy was hidden from view during their conversation.

FOR A FEW MOMENTS, a third person had been a party to their discussion – a person who stood in the shadows in the hall beyond the study door, which had not been properly closed by the duchess.

It was Mary, Isabella's maid. Yet, her status

made her as unnoticeable as any other servant in the household. Neither the footmen nor a passing maid paid the least bit of attention to her. In her plain dress and cap, with her less-than-distinguished features, who would ever notice her? Who was she compared to anyone? She was just a lady's maid who was *slightly* out of place.

CHAPTER 13

"*D*o you remember that baronet I spoke of from Beyton Dale – the gentleman from the green picnic?" Lady Diana gushed to her friend. "He is here, dear Isabella."

Isabella did not immediately react to the news, nor did she react as Diana expected her to. She was still reeling from the events of the evening, so far – being presented at court, the celebration dinner, and, now the ball. She was not sure if she was capable of displaying anything other than a smile on her face. She had been forcing herself to wear a smile all evening.

Although her expression was not as genuine as she might have wished, she *was* truly, genuinely happy for Diana, who was beaming in rapturous delight at every detail. From the music, to the punch, and the great number of people who had arrived, she was radiant in this moment, for which she had prepared all of her life.

"Perhaps you did not hear what I said over the music? The baronet from Beyton Dale – he is *here*. The gentleman who is not strictly good looking but rather charismatic?" Diana exclaimed. "I am so pleased that he was invited, he *is* an acquaintance of our family, even though his rank is rather low for the company. No matter his rank, he is here, and he has been making inquiries about you, is that not delightful?"

"About *me*?"

She peered at Isabella, as all around the young women, well-wishers, and invitees to the London mansion laughed, chatted, and took their turn dancing if they were so inclined. The music was loud, and the voices combined into a cacophony. In every direction that Isabella turned, there were great numbers of fashionably dressed people. The evening was a great success, but it was all so overwhelming. The news of the baronet's arrival, and his interest in her, were more than she was capable of considering, at least for the moment. She quickly realised that Lady Diana would not be content until she had the hoped-for reaction from her. Isabella did feel a sense of relief that a gentleman – bother the rank – was making inquiries about her. For that, she *was* happy.

"That is good news. Did you say he was from Beyton Dale? Would I remember him?"

"I doubt that you would recall him." Lady Diana chatted in her bubbly manner, answering Isabella's question. "It was the day that my brother accompanied us on the picnic. I am astonished that he, the baronet, Colonel Sir William Gardiner, is bold enough to make enquiries at all."

"Perhaps he is the courageous sort."

"Yes, how thrilling … Oh, there he is." Lady

Diana gestured subtly to a gentleman, wearing a military uniform. "My, what a dashing figure he is in his officer's crimson."

The gentleman was wearing the gold-trimmed red uniform of a colonel. His auburn hair shone in the candlelight, and his smile, a wide kind of expression showed that he was not reserved, as he strode towards Isabella and Lady Diana. With a bow, he greeted Lady Diana who giggled in a most improper but charming way before she made the introduction between Isabella and the young man who smiled at Isabella.

As she gazed at him, she was surprised to find she recognised him as the young man she had seen with his black dog from the window at Hardwick Manor. She examined the red of his uniform, the glimmer of the buttons and the hilt of his sword. Could he have been the mysterious person in the garden? Did she imagine that she saw the same unmistakable hue of crimson? Were they his footsteps that she had heard growing faint with distance in the twilight? As she observed him, she was filled with an insatiable desire to ask him if he had ever visited the gardens at Hardwick Manor, but she chose to remain silent, until she decided with a smile, she had ample opportunity to ask the question. With her curiosity well suppressed for the moment, she set about the rather agreeable task of observing him.

He was taller than her, but not by much. She noted that his shoulders and neck were broad, as was his chin and face, but not to a disagreeable degree. He was built sturdily and strong, as though he was a man who wore the title of a gentleman but who could be relied upon to use his stature if necessary.

His green eyes sparkled as he spoke to her in a manner that she found to be more pleasant and elegant than his muscular build would suggest. "Lady Isabella, it is a great honour to be introduced to you. As Lady Diana has told you, I am Colonel Gardiner."

"Colonel Gardiner," Isabella said as she curtseyed.

"There is an Irish reel starting … you should dance, Colonel Gardiner," Lady Diana suggested cheerfully. "I am sure there are … *many* young ladies who would be delighted to accompany you."

Isabella agreed with Diana's summary of the man so far. The colonel was an engaging figure, even if his features were not as aristocratic as His Grace's were, nor was he as tall, she observed, as he smiled at her, his face softened by the expression.

"Ah, but there are none as fair as the two who stand before me now," the colonel replied gallantly. "Lady Isabella, would you do me the great honour of accepting this dance with me?" he asked, offering his arm to Isabella.

Isabella inclined her head in acceptance with a smile.

"I hope that you do not find me forward," the colonel continued, "but I have a terrible habit of speaking my mind. A trait that I am told could offend a lady not used to the rough manners of an officer," he said as he leaned closer to her, a necessity due to the crowded ballroom. Or did he wish to be near to her? He did claim that he was forward. Of that she had no doubt, and Lady Diana had said so, as well.

"What do you wish to say to me that could cause offence?" she asked, as she struggled to be heard over the music and the laughter of the couples who were assembling for the dance.

"I wish to say that I have wanted to meet you for some time … one day last summer I chanced upon Lady Diana and her family on the green in Beyton Dale. You were with them, but of course, we could not be introduced because you were in mourning," he answered and assumed his place opposite her.

There was not an opportunity to answer him, as he beamed at her, a wide grin that was rather captivating.

"I also could not offer you my condolences on your loss, which I do now." His smile dimmed momentarily.

Again, the room was too full of noise to reply, but Isabella inclined her head in thanks, and his smile returned. The music played, and she was swept along with the other dancers, as she recalled the steps to the reel. Her partner was remarkably skilled. He moved quickly and correctly, clapping in all the appropriate places, and finding every opportunity to smile in her direction. He acted as though she was the most beautiful woman in the room and that he was elated she had chosen him for a dance partner. She would never acknowledge it, but it was what his smiles and his attention seemed to indicate. He was a gentleman of low rank, according to Lady Diana, but what care did Isabella have for rank?

Especially, following the letter she received from her solicitor, several weeks before her presentation.

Isabella had been sitting in her room, waiting for Mary to help her style her hair for the evening meal.

There had been a knock at the door, and Mary had appeared, curling irons in hand. Her face, however, had not looked like that of someone whose only concern was a tasteful curl or two. Her face had told of concern, even shock, and she had been pale.

"Mary, are you well?" Isabella had asked in concern, as she turned towards the woman.

"Oh, yes, my lady, ahhhh, oh, dear."

"Whatever is the matter?"

Mary had looked sideways as if she wished she could escape the words. "Oh, Miss. I was just on my way here, and I passed the master's study. I heard your name, so I lingered a little to hear what might be said—"

"Yes?"

She would have gone further, but there had been another quick knock at the door, and Diana had come in holding a thick cream envelope.

It had been a letter, just delivered from Isabella's solicitor, and Mary's potential news was forgotten as Isabella read the lines.

Her solicitor had apologised that he had let time pass but had excused his delay by saying he had hoped to be able to write better news, a hope that had not been fulfilled. He broke the news to her that her half-brother was to be charged with murder. What turned the news from bad to horrendous was that he would be charged with the murder of their own father ...

Could it be true, that her brother had murdered her father?

Charles had fled ... he could be hiding anywhere. His threats to her were still fresh in her memory...

For her part, as soon as she saw Isabella's reaction, Mary must have realised the news that she had been about to impart was also contained in the letter. The expression on her face was evident. She must have felt some relief at not having to be the one to break it to her mistress, although to Isabella, she seemed shocked to have the overheard conversation confirmed in so decisive a manner. Mary had given her a knowing look and lowered her head.

Since that moment, the awful contents of the letter had not ever really left her mind.

How could she forget such news, or the dreadful consequences and the anger should the charges be proven? Moreover, how could she hope to find a gentleman who would wish to marry her with such a sordid scandal hanging over her head? The best she could wish for was a quick marriage before rumours began to circulate about her half-brother. Such rumours would destroy her chances of finding a match or a position if she were to stay in England. Could she remain in her beloved country?

Dancing and turning, and feeling the music carry her, she attempted to remain light and airy. She had little time. This was her chance to find a match before it was too late.

"Lady Isabella, are you not enjoying the dancing?" the colonel asked as he spun her around.

Isabella felt terrible to lie, but she had no other choice. "Forgive me, I am not practiced at the Irish reel. I was trying to recall the steps."

"You dance better than any woman I have

had the pleasure of accompanying this evening."

She wanted to believe him. His complement was given with such sincerity that she was willing to accept that he truly admired her, as they came together again in the centre of the room. The colonel was far more graceful then she had presumed such a soldier would be, and he never stopped smiling at her. As she danced with him, she could almost forget her troubles concerning Charles.

When the dance came to an end, she felt the gaze of several of the gentlemen nearby. She could not ignore the attention that she was receiving – especially from her dancing partner, who beamed at her in pride. "It looks as if others also believe I am the luckiest man at the ball." He smiled at her. "If I do not ask you for another dance right away, I shall lose you to some other man."

"I appreciate your kindness." She gave him a brief nod. "I wish that every gentleman spoke as you do, sincerely and without reservation."

"You may rely on me for that, if nothing else, Lady Isabella. It would be my sincere honour to partner you for another dance this evening, as soon as you consider it seemly. I do not want to appear overly forward, even for me, and I hesitate to set the tongues wagging about us, in case it reflects badly on you."

She found this consideration presented him in a genuinely good light, and she saw a man who could be kind, as well as bold. She hoped that she would find him to be even more honest, if she could find the best manner in which to broach the subject of her having seen him at Hardwick Manor. It was not her place to ask him his reasons or to seek an explanation, but she needed to put her mind at rest.

In the end, she decided honesty would be best and would get her to the truth in the most direct manner. As he escorted her back towards Diana, she forced her voice to be light. "I must confess, Colonel, that I think I have seen you before, albeit from a distance, so I may be mistaken."

"Oh?" He paused and looked at her enquiringly.

"Well." She hesitated to make her words sound unplanned. "Several days after the picnic on the village green, I thought I saw a man, who I now believe was you on the grounds of Hardwick Manor."

He seemed genuinely puzzled. "I don't think —" he began, just at the same time as Isabella said:

"You were with a coach and accompanied by a dog ..."

His puzzlement disappeared immediately, replaced by an almost bashful grin.

"Oh! Yes!" he exclaimed. "That dashed dog, Zeus! He was the reason for my trespass, which I admit, I thought I had quite gotten away with."

His eyes sparkled like those of a naughty boy caught stealing apples in an orchard.

"Zeus is my dog. That day he followed a hare through the forest near Hardwick Manor, and I thought him lost for good. As I was passing the manor, hanging out of the coach window like a complete dunderhead, looking for the foolish animal, I heard him barking from inside the grounds. Well, I instructed my man to drive to the front door directly, so we could enquire about looking for him, as any gentleman would, but as luck would have it, the miscreant recognised the carriage and ran up to us as soon as we were at the edge of the formal gardens. It was getting late, and I thought that perhaps I could just take him and leave as quietly as we had arrived. As soon as I stepped out of the coach, he thought it a fine game to make two or three sprints around me before I could get him to obey. I looked towards the house, but fortunately the windows seemed dark and the pair of us remained unobserved. Or … so I thought until this evening."

He laughed. "You must have thought me very odd, Lady Isabella."

"Oh, I quite understand how quickly circumstances can change, and how easy it is to attribute a false reason to what is observed but not understood," Isabella replied.

In fact, she was suddenly filled with a wonderful sense of relief, and a great weight had been lifted from her chest. It *was* the colonel she had seen! That meant it could not have been her half-brother. That also made it all the more ridiculous to assume he had been in the garden on that autumn evening. Suddenly, the expensive ribbon of a colour favoured by Lady Diana that she had found became what it had been all along: a lost trinket from a past summer's day and nothing more ominous. Her mood lifted so suddenly it was if the sun had come out, right in the middle of the evening. She immediately felt sunny, and light, too.

She looked up at the colonel with a hint of mischief on her face. "So, I can assume the manor's silverware collection is no longer in danger."

For a split second he appeared surprised at her boldness, and then he began to laugh heartily. "I do hope you will keep my temporary lack of etiquette between us, Lady Isabella. My fate is in your hands now."

Her answer was a warm and genuine smile.

After dancing with the colonel, Isabella was partnered with the second son of an earl, and then a viscount. While dancing with both of these gentlemen she felt the steady gaze of Colonel Gardiner, whose admiration was not extinguished when she was compelled by good manners and convention to seek other dancing partners. They both understood that dancing exclusively with the same gentleman sent a message to society that a couple was either secretly engaged or had already announced their plans for matrimony. Despite the necessity to find an advantageous match, she did not wish to expose herself to gossip by dancing with one single man, and she found the other gentlemen all amiable and polite.

However, she found she was scrutinizing every man who asked her to dance and comparing them to His Grace. She found each man wanting in some way as they had held her close for the dance. Why did she hold the duke in such high regard, when he had scarcely spoken to her beyond the expected civilities? What was in his eyes, his character, or his confident manner that made her find fault in nearly every other man who sought her company?

DIANA'S PREDICTIONS had come true, and Isabella was one of the most popular girls at the ball, dancing each and every dance. In doing so, she failed to observe the close scrutiny to which she was being subjected by all and sundry.

Lady Diana's popularity matched Isabella's. Isabella was the whispered beauty of the evening, in her glittering, golden sarsenet-encased ivory gown, but Lady Diana was just as sought after a young lady in her own right. Being the sister of a wealthy and respected duke, she was considered by many to be one of the most well-regarded young ladies in all of London. She had good connections and was in possession of a considerable dowry. When those attributes were considered, along with her youthful exuberance and her natural charm, she was as much a draw as Isabella was, although gentlemen of higher rank made up the majority of these admirers. Diana drew the attention of dukes and heirs to earldoms, as Isabella was doted on by second sons and lower ranking aristocrats. Notwithstanding this, by any standard, each woman was having a splendidly successful night.

That observation was remarked on by the woman who had orchestrated the entire affair, to her son.

"Your sister will be engaged by June, mark my words," the dowager duchess proclaimed to Matthew.

"I never doubted that she would be well received," he replied. As the duchess watched him, she noticed that he was speaking about his sister – but that his eyes never left Isabella.

"What of Lady Isabella?" she asked as she fanned herself languorously.

"Lady Isabella? I have not noticed her this evening."

"Oh, is that so?" The duchess raised an eyebrow at her son. "She has not been without a partner for the entirety of the evening. I was certain that you would ask her to dance. It is fitting that you should – this is her coming-out ball, after all. As her guardian, it is your duty to dance with her, and not permit that baronet to claim her attention. If I had thought for a moment that you would show no inclination to asking her to dance, I would have never allowed the baronet to attend. Any gentleman would have welcomed the addition of a rival to stir his interest. Perhaps I was mistaken that you would be swayed by a rival?"

He did not answer. Instead, the duchess watched as he stared in Isabella's direction. She was now dancing with Colonel Gardiner again. With a quick bow, the duke turned from his mother and started walking towards the room's entrance.

· · ·

HIS LEAVING WAS NOTICED by one other person in the room. Isabella wondered why he had not asked her to dance. It would have been the proper and polite thing to do, but she should have understood by now that the Duke of Devonshire cared not enough for her to do so.

He had not asked her to dance nor did she expect that he would now, even though she had hoped he would. Since she was already forming a bad habit of comparing the gentlemen she met at the ball to the duke, she found that Colonel Gardiner – unlike His Grace – was content, to the point of enthusiasm, to be in her company. When she stared into the bright-green eyes of the baronet, she felt compelled to smile. If she must accept a man, who did not possess the traits that she wished for in a match, or who did not embody *all* of her ideals of what a man should be, why should it matter how he compared to His Grace? She would accept the man who admired her greatly and be satisfied that he did not treat her as a debt to be repaid.

She glanced towards the doorway of the ballroom. For a mere moment, she thought she saw the duke turn back towards her, and their eyes locked for a second before he was gone. In a room as crowded as it was, she questioned whether she had truly observed him, or caught his eye. With a wistful look at the place where he had stood, she realised that he had left.

He had not danced with her nor spoken more than a few words to her all evening, unlike Colonel Gardiner. She had just turned towards her shorter, uniformed companion, who was waiting beside her, when suddenly the duke was by her side, offering his hand for a dance. She realised that he must have left the room to bring him to her via the outside corridor to circumvent the crowd and the press of dancers.

"Lady Isabella, might I have the honour?" he intoned, the invitation to dance echoed in his voice and posture.

Colonel Gardiner bowed to the duke, acknowledging his request to relinquish his intended partner. In something of a blur, Isabella found herself standing before the duke, as the orchestra master announced a German Waltz.

She wondered briefly whether the duke regretted having chosen this moment to ask her to dance, or whether he had chosen it specifically. The waltz had been popular for a number of years now, but it was still considered quite "new" in many of the staider ballroom circles. Despite the well-known hostess, Lady Mary Bentinck's having introduced what she had called "a new and beautiful dance," there were still many chaperones and society mothers who disapproved (just as Lady Diana had mentioned) of the fact that the dance was for couples – and that its alternating fast and slow, whirling nature had caused more than one young lady to swoon into the arms of her dancing partner.

Nevertheless, Isabella felt a thrill of excitement as she and the duke faced each other, and she smiled at him. He passed his arms along hers and held her by the elbows. She moved to mirror his position, and the music began. He turned her in a circle, towards the left – taking the place that the couple before them had vacated, so that the entire circle of pairs of dancers moved at the same time and in the same direction.

Even though it was an altogether graceful and charming spectacle, Isabella found it hard to concentrate on the display, or the other dancers. Her position meant she was as close to the duke as she had only experienced twice – and certainly never in public. She could smell his cologne – a woody, slightly spicy scent that she recognised from the library at the manor. It elicited an unexpected physical response in her. She felt her heart jolt inside her chest, beating wildly. Oh, she had been hoping for this moment since arriving at the ball!

She noticed how the lights from the chandeliers made his light-coloured hair appear fairer and it shone as if gilded. At the same time as she was chiding herself for having these unashamedly girlish notions, she realised that she was acknowledging her feelings for him. Was she *truly* in love with the duke?

"Are you enjoying the ball, Lady Isabella?" He broke into her thoughts with his murmured question.

"I am," she replied. *Honestly*, she thought, *I do hope we are not going to speak as if we hardly know one another.*

"How do you find the evening, Your Grace?" she asked, hoping to open an opportunity for a more satisfying exchange.

"It is a well-organised and pleasant event," he answered politely, if somewhat unexpectedly. But his next words caused her heart to beat even faster. "I must admit that until now, I *had* found it rather unremarkable, but you are a charming and graceful dancer, Lady Isabella. Of course, I should have expected this having observed how elegantly you ride."

Two compliments in one moment! Isabella allowed herself to hope he may feel something other than duty towards her after all! She lifted her eyes to his face, but it remained calm and impassive.

"You are too kind." She managed the expected response.

She thought he smiled, but then, the tempo of the music changed, and they were swept into a faster series of movements. She lowered her head again, so as to be sure she remained on her feet. Any loss of balance would be interpreted as clumsy at best and coquettish at worst!

After that, there was not another moment for dialogue, and when the dance finished, he released her and bowed in gratitude. Had she imagined that his fingers had swept her hand as he unloosed his hold on her? Time was moving so slowly at that point – she could not be certain. She was aware of her racing pulse and the blood pounding in her ears. He turned to lead her towards the side of the dance floor, but stopped as he saw Colonel Gardiner approaching through the crowd, obviously intent on claiming Isabella again for the next dance.

The duke turned towards Isabella, obscuring her view of the colonel. "Lady Isabella." It was astonishing how many different meanings he could convey by only saying her name. This time, however, it was to wish her adieu, and she was certain there was an undertone of regret in his voice. Or was there not?

For her part, she only bowed her head.

Then, the next moment, Colonel Gardiner was at her side and, she felt a sinking feeling in the pit of her stomach as the coldest of realities reminded her that he was her most suitable prospect. She recognised how ungrateful she was being and chided herself for having hoped for something more.

Then, once again, she allowed herself to be swept up in the exuberance of the music and the night as the musicians began to play the next dance. Although she enjoyed the dancing and merriment, she could not help but sneak a glimpse about the room in search of the duke throughout the evening.

CHAPTER 14

Colonel Gardiner soon proved himself to be bolder than even Lady Diana had presumed. After the evening of the ball, and without any obvious sign that he was intimidated by the duke, the colonel began to visit Isabella. The presence of a baronet in the drawing room was rather shocking to the Duchess of Devonshire – she was not exactly in favour of the budding friendship between Isabella and the baronet – but she recognised that Isabella's position meant that she could not afford to discourage a potential suitor. The ball had shown her that it would take more than a little rivalry to force her son to acknowledge his feelings for the young woman – if that ever happened. With the exception of a ball or other large gatherings, where such an acquaintance could easily go unnoticed, decorum dictated that she must at least extend the invitation if these people were in town – which Colonel Gardiner most certainly was – and now he showed no sign of leaving, not while he was being welcomed so warmly into the mansion of the Duke of Devonshire.

The duchess felt uneasy encouraging the man when her own hopeful preference for Isabella lay elsewhere; however, she indulged her daughter and Isabella, as the young man was something of a war hero.

THE DUKE OCCUPIED himself with his own affairs either at home or away when the baronet called, as was the right of his superior rank and title. He did not need to be told by his mother, who was maintaining a watchful eye on the proceedings, that Isabella was enjoying the attention of the strapping young man. He was aware of the progress of the acquaintance, although he doubted Isabella would accept a man such as Colonel Gardiner. He was not a bad sort, but he was, so he thought, far too predictable for a woman such as Isabella to consider – predictable and traditional. The duke knew the baronet's family well; their families had been long acquainted. He knew of their strict adherence to convention, and he also knew that Isabella was not a woman whose unconventional upbringing or her own manner of living would fit into those conventions – despite outward appearances.

He smiled to himself as he added up a column of figures in his account ledger, when he thought of her confession that she rode astride, or of the time he had found her in the garden, or again one of the earlier memories of her insistence that she pay her maid, even if she had no money of her own. She was a singular woman, indeed. Most certainly the baronet would have a difficult time breaking her of those habits – like breaking a wild horse. The duke doubted that it could be done, and so he did not worry about the acquaintance. He was convinced, and rightly so, that Isabella, herself, would soon see that Colonel Gardiner, for all his charm and heroism, was not the man for her.

This led him to a question that had been floating around his head since the ball, where he had watched her dance with other gentlemen. *Who was the right man for her?* He did not have long to ponder that question, as a rapping on the door brought a visitor to his study.

"That officious colonel has returned," the dowager duchess stated grumpily.

"I should not worry about Gardiner, Mother. Let him have his fun. He shall be off soon enough to find a more suitable bride – one who fits better to the model his family has set," Matthew replied, as he turned his attention back to the columns of numbers on the page in front of him.

"Matthew, did you not hear a word I said to you? The baronet is here again. This makes the second time this week he has strolled into my house and ensconced himself in my drawing room. I do not know how I can dissuade him from returning. When we are in Derbyshire, his mother and I are on speaking terms and his father was a regular at our house for balls and hunting parties, but ..."

"All young men test their boundaries now and again."

"He is a nice enough young man. He has served his country valiantly and would make a good husband for a young woman of his own rank. I do not say this out of spite, but his family has some prestige in Beyton Dale. Perhaps that has gone to his head? Or could it be the gold insignia and braids on his uniform? He is a colonel ... could he be so presumptuous to assume that his rank in the army has lifted him up from his proper place in society?

My word, but he has become bold for a Gardiner."

She sighed as if she really did not understand. "His father was so reliable, so dependable … but this young man, he seems to be quite a different man altogether," she lamented before sitting in a chair, her face set in a scowl.

Matthew dismissed his mother's concerns. "He is by no means going to go against anything his mother has to say about his marriage prospects, or what is expected of him. Duty and honour will win the day. When it comes to the end, he is a Gardiner, and he will fall in line with whatever his mother wishes for him and his duty to his title. He will not want a woman who possesses the slightest hint of independence. Not for a wife."

"Matthew, it is a different world. I am many years your elder and I can see that. Perhaps you are incapable of seeing the world as it has become because you spend far less time among society. You, and your labouring like an estate agent. Have you no care for what is happening beyond the door of this study?"

"I assure you that the world has not changed so greatly that I should have any reason to concern myself with Sir William Gardiner, even if he rightly calls himself a colonel these days."

The duchess was incensed. "Dismiss him if you wish, but he is not the kind of man to be content to remain in the low position into which he was born. Nor are many of the young men who have returned from the continent these days. The war has changed gentlemen and changed all of society. There was a time when a man such as he would hardly be welcome at a dinner given by a viscount, but here he is in our house and I cannot ask him to leave. I would be shunned like a pariah if I were to treat an officer in such a manner in war time. Believe me, Matthew he knows this, and so does every other young man in a red uniform these days. Second sons are acting bold as brass … what will it be next – merchants and tradesmen taking tea in our house?"

"Mother, there is no reason for concern. Lady Isabella will soon tire of him, and then he will be on his way again."

"What if you are entirely wrong?"

"She could never be content as the wife of such a man."

"She is beautiful – she possesses a charm that many gentlemen would find compelling. Perhaps so compelling that her regrettable circumstances pose no hindrance to a match."

"I am not wrong – how could I be? If she does not rescind her favour from the colonel, then the scandal concerning her half-brother will dampen any regard he may have for her. Colonel Gardiner will not flaunt convention by marrying the sister of a murderer and a debt-ridden card shark. His family possesses neither the wealth nor the rank to overcome such an impediment."

"I would not be so sure," the older woman said. "He appears to be rather taken with her."

WHILE THE DUCHESS was warning her son about the dangers of the close acquaintance that was forming at an alarming rate between Colonel Gardiner and Lady Isabella, the colonel was telling his small audience of Lady Diana and Lady Isabella a harrowing but funny tale of one of his many youthful adventures.

Lady Diana laughed out loud, her joy uninhibited. Isabella gasped in an attempt to appear shocked at the outcome of the story told by the colonel. In truth, she had seen far too much of the world to be truly shocked by many things, but in the drawing room with a would-be suitor in attendance, she had to play the part of a demure lady – even if that part was wearing as thin as a pair of dancing slippers during a ball.

Isabella knew that he was not particularly well-read, but she imagined that she could do far worse than a colonel, especially with her brother still wanted for the murder of her father (a subject that she hoped would never become known in London). She enjoyed the colonel's enthusiasm and merry stories, but she did not believe that she could ever truly share any moments of closeness with him, not that she minded. If she found a man who would marry her, and who was not tedious or vile, then she would make concessions. It was all that could be done to secure her future. She had to accept that or advertise for a position in the colonies as a governess or a companion. When she thought of becoming a wife and the mistress of her own house, especially one in Beyton Dale where she could be near Hardwick Manor, she smiled. Surely, she could endure the colonel's less-than-ideal traits, if she could be near the duchess and Diana and retain her maid, Mary.

THE DUCHESS RETURNED to the drawing room, grateful that none of her own close acquaintances were in attendance to witness the regrettable scene that was playing out in her home and under her roof. Despite her son's dismissal of her concerns, her anger remained. The very idea that a baronet should be entertained in the house of a duke was improper to her. The difference in class was far too vast to be surmounted, despite the familiarity of the acquaintance. She was angry that Colonel Gardiner was surely exploiting this familiarity to his advantage, as he regaled her daughter and her ward with another outrageous tale. *Oh, she should never have invited him to the ball,* she chided herself. If she were at all introspective, she would have seen this as justice served, because, in reality, she had hoped the colonel would prompt some feeling of jealousy in her son. Luckily, the duchess was not often given to such regrets. Standing poised and prepared to make an entrance, she thought of what she would say to the young man. It was becoming apparent that she would have to remind him of his proper place, but her plans were delayed by the appearance of a footman at her side.

"Your Grace, a letter has just arrived for

Lady Isabella," the footman spoke in a low tone to her. His mannerisms and voice were carefully regulated to cause the least amount of disruption to his mistress.

The duchess did not immediately recognise the handwriting on the note as she wondered who could be writing to the young woman. She knew of no one who maintained correspondence with her – Lady Isabella had no family, to speak of. The Viscount of Wharton certainly did not. He was far too involved in his own affairs to concern himself with the troubles of a distant relation.

"Lady Isabella," she said as she handed the letter to Isabella.

ISABELLA GLANCED at the letter and was suddenly overcome with a wave of powerful emotions, none of them good. The handwriting was her solicitor's and the bold slant of the address could mean only one thing: the letter had been sent in haste. That did not bode well, but she tried to maintain her composure under the scrutiny of the duchess, Lady Diana and Colonel Gardiner.

"It is not bad news, I trust. The colour has drained from your face – are you well?" Lady Diana asked, oblivious to any reason why her friend could be reacting to a letter that sat un-opened but clutched in her hand.

"If you will excuse me," Isabella said as she rose from her chair. "I must attend to this at once, and would prefer to read this through myself before disclosing its contents. Would you send Mary upstairs with tea? I am in need of it … if you will pardon me, I must be going …"

Rushing from the room, she did not look back. She needed to be alone to read the letter, hastily penned by the solicitor. From the weight of the letter, she had a terrible suspicion that not only was the news contained beneath the wax seal not good, but that it was a lengthy missive filled with not a single thing she wanted to read.

Once she reached the haven of her room, she flung herself across her bed, feeling her heart flutter inside of her chest.

Isabella opened the letter. When she read the first words, her breathing became laboured, and she forced herself not to faint.

CHAPTER 15

*H*er life was changing and there was nothing she could do to stop it. Her half-brother had been found. He was alive. She gasped as she read the lines, "he had been arrested." She could not escape the scandal, not anymore.

At the same time as Isabella was refusing to come downstairs for the evening meal – she was thrown into grief and panic about her half-brother – the news that he would face a trial for his crimes was already travelling at a swift rate around the salons, drawing rooms, and dining tables of London society. Charles Thornton, Viscount (and he who should have been the next earl) of Chatham had been arrested in Whitechapel, London, probably trying to hide, at a less-than-reputable pub, the Red Rooster Inn. His arrest would not have been noteworthy in any way except for his rank and his connections with the gentlemen of upper-class society. How many young men had lost vast sums to him at the clubs? How many loans had he refused to pay, and debts had he not honoured?

News that he was a suspected murderer, of his own father no less, was repeated in hushed tones and not-so-whispered voices that evening as Isabella sequestered herself away from it all. Her maid relayed what was being said in the kitchen down below, among the footmen, who moved between the great houses of the lords and lady's unseen as they carried notes, missives, and invitations.

In her anguish, Isabella knew that any hope for a future as a respectable member of society was over. She had not spoken to Colonel Gardiner about the subject of her half-brother. The reason why she had chosen not to confide in him was not out of fear – but of humiliation. What was there to be said about the matter that would have helped the situation? With charges pending against her half-brother, the dispersion of the estate would soon be settled. Still, her annuity had been arranged and her dowry was restored, but at what price? Who would have her?

COLONEL GARDINER WAS NOT DISTURBED by the gossip that reached his ears that night – at least not in the manner the Duke of Devonshire had predicted. The baronet moved to put his own future in a better standing, as he put his plan in place while the duke's house was still in a quiet chaos. It was a plan that he had been forming for a long time. Yet at that hour, at dinner, no one yet knew of it. That would come later.

Mary did not act as a lady's maid that afternoon or later that night, so she was able to pick up the rumours and gossip in the servants' hall. The contents of the letter did not startle her, as she had been well aware of the villainy of Isabella's half-brother for some time. But, she knew something more – something that she intended to tell her mistress, who was weeping by the fireside.

After several trips up the servants' stairs, bringing tea, and sending word to the duchess that Isabella had suddenly taken ill with a headache and then downstairs again to reassure Lady Diana and the duchess that Isabella was in no danger, Mary sat with her mistress. She wished she could help her forget her present troubles by trying to act as a friend, but she knew that all she could do was tell her mistress the truth.

"Mary, what is to be done? Who will marry me now that Charles has been arrested? Who would want to make such a connection? I shall be forced to find work somewhere, so far away that no one knows my name or Charles's crime. I suppose that I could set myself up in a distant county, to the north, perhaps? I know what to do, but I cannot remain here. Not for another day. My leaving will also relieve the duke of my burden and any more shame and gossip caused by my half-brother's actions – that is certain."

"It gives me no joy to hear you say that … but I will not say that you are wrong, I am afraid, my lady," Mary replied with a sad expression on her face. "You are right, most decidedly so. His Grace will be pleased, I am sorry to say."

"Mary, do you mean that His Grace will be *glad* I am gone?"

"Oh, my lady, I did not mean to say that, not like that."

"Tell me – what would give you cause to say such a thing?" Isabella implored the woman.

Mary's face was twisted in anguish. "I never

like to admit to listening when you or the family is speaking. It is not my place to listen, but I did hear the duke say something that upset me. It bothered me when I heard it said, as it bothers me to see you in such a state. I tried to tell you before, but then you got that first letter about your half-brother and—"

"What did he say?" Isabella interrupted. "Mary, you must tell me."

"He said that you were his duty, and his responsibility. He swore to protect you from your half-brother. He knew about him, all about him … but that was not so dreadful. He hired footmen and sentries, he said. I know it to be true. I saw them about the place at Hardwick Manor."

"He said that I was a duty? A responsibility?" Isabella said slowly, each word magnifying in her mind as she said it.

"His Grace vowed to see you married to a gentleman. That was how he described his debt to your departed father, God rest his lordship's soul. He was to see you clothed and fed and married off to any gentlemen who would take you off his hands."

For a second, Isabella seemed vulnerable, her feelings as raw and unchecked as if she was not of noble upbringing, but then she quickly regained her composure. "I should not be surprised. He will not miss me, not at all."

"What of the young lady, and her mother the Duchess of Devonshire? They will miss you something terrible."

"They may, as I will them, but they will soon find other amusements."

"It may be too bold to ask, my lady, but what of that nice colonel? You could marry him, could you not?"

"He would not have me, not now. I dare not impose upon his kindness or embarrass him by presuming upon our acquaintance."

"What will you do, then?" Mary asked her mistress.

Isabella wiped the tears from her face and looked at her maid, with determination in her eyes, she said: "I will tell you what I am going to do. I am going to the north, far away from London and anyone who knows me or anything about me. Come with me if you wish. I have the means to afford a modest living for a time. It is not much, but it shall provide us with food and clothing if we are careful."

"The north?"

"I may become a governess ... I may leave England ... I do not yet know, but I do know that I cannot stay here. Not when I am a burden to the people that I hold dear in my heart ... a debt to be paid. It pains me that *he* knew of my half-brother, knew more than I did, and he did not seek to inform me of his knowledge – or offer me the slightest comfort. Instead, he sought to see me wed to any man who would have me. I shall not impose upon His Grace a day longer. I shall miss his mother and his dear sister, but I must leave, I cannot stay. Not when I am not wanted. Will you come with me, Mary? Shall I have you for a travel companion?"

CHAPTER 16

$\mathcal{M}$ary did not answer. Isabella presumed her silence was her agreement, so she said, "Mary, please prepare my things. I do not want anyone to know of my arrangements – not until I am gone and safely away from the scandal Charles has caused."

With her decision made, Isabella felt a great sadness, and a weight settled in her chest. But, what else could she do? She could not remain in London where she faced scandal. She did not want to poison Lady Diana's chances for marriage with their association nor did she wish to take advantage of the duke's kindness for one more day. Not when his charity was no longer necessary. She now had a modest annuity. It would never afford a grand house or servants, other than Mary, but it might furnish Isabella with a cottage, and perhaps a garden of her very own. That would have to do; it was not much, but it was the best she could hope for, after she left the London home of the Duke of Devonshire. She realised that she did not care at all for Colonel Gardiner, she was certain from the lack of sadness she felt at the prospect of never seeing him again.

What was astonishing was how she felt when she considered that she would never see His Grace again. Unexpectedly, that realisation hurt her deeply, causing an ache that was more profound and far more powerful than she could ever have imagined. She had to remind herself that she was a burden to him, now more than ever before. It was as she had long feared. No matter what she thought may have passed between them: the laughter, the conversation, the looks, and her excitement that he caused when he was close to her. All of that was not real, it never had been. It was best to forget about it and continue with her life in a faraway place. She was accustomed to travelling, to seeing new places and strange ports. She knew how to make her way in the world – her father had taught her that. It was a lesson she never dreamed she would need.

Until now.

ISABELLA MIGHT HAVE SLIPPED AWAY in the dead of night – if she had been so inclined, or before dawn, but she was not the sort to slink away without saying goodbye in such a manner. Long after the house had grown silent, and after she believed all would surely be in bed, she made a decision. She would leave a letter in the duke's study. He could read it to his sister and his mother if he so chose. It was far better than facing a tearful goodbye from the women of the Danvers family, who would attempt to change her mind, of that she was certain (and if she were honest, rather happy about). However, nothing could alter her path. Not now. She was not going to be a burden, not when she could manage a living for herself and her maid for a few months, until she could find a situation or, if things came to the worst, Mary could seek another position. She hoped Mary would understand, as she recalled their conversation from earlier in the day. She had sworn Mary to secrecy while asking her to begin her packing. Now she stood with the letter in her hand – a letter that had been painful to write.

My Lord Duke,

I am forever indebted to Your Grace for your generosity and the kindness shown to me by your family. It is with sadness that cannot be measured that I write this letter and beg your understanding. When you read this, I shall be gone. I cannot bear the thought of leaving, but I must do what I am able to secure my future.

It has become impossible for me to bear another

moment of the shame that will torment me every day, and if I remain among kind people, who do not deserve the stain that association with me will surely bring. I feel I can only manage this terrible weight if I leave to seek employment somewhere where my story is unknown. This decision is not taken with any degree of impulsiveness but has been thoroughly considered in every way. I sincerely offer you my gratitude and wish that you, your mother, and sister may know every happiness.

She sealed the letter and looked at the trunk by her bed. She felt a lump rising in her throat. This was difficult, far more than she would have suspected. Leaving Lady Diana without saying goodbye was terrible, leaving the dowager duchess was even worse, but leaving the Duke of Devonshire, that was devastating.

She quietly mounted the stairs to the servants' quarters and tapped on Mary's door. She knew her maid would be preparing her own belongings in preparation for their trip. Mary opened the door and beckoned her inside. Isabella stepped into the small room, and in a low voice she said, "Please be ready to leave as soon as the kitchen staff begin to stir, Mary. In that way we will not have to ask to have a door opened, and should we meet a servant, they will not dare question our being about."

"Yes, my lady," was all Mary could manage. She was also very sorry to be leaving Hardwick Manor.

Isabella bade her maid goodnight and left the room, quietly closing the door behind her. She descended the stairs again and turned in the direction of the duke's study.

She barely recalled standing on the landing, with her fingers running along the ink of his title on the paper, nor did she remember walking along the hall and past the drawing room. It was silent in the gloom of the hall, but Isabella noticed a glow of the candlelight from inside the study. Her heart began to race. She had not expected that he would be awake at this hour. After all, it was well after midnight. She listened closely and shrank into the shadows as she heard two voices, both masculine.

At first, she could not understand the muffled words, but then she started when she heard the duke's voice grow louder, and his next question was clear.

"Are you sure that she has gone? Have you looked in every room of the house? Wake every footman, we must find her!" the duke barked orders in a gruff tone of voice.

"Yes, Your Grace, at once." She heard a man say in response, and only seconds later, a footman barrelled past her, not seeing her in the darkness.

The letter gripped tightly in her trembling fingers, she hesitated to move from beyond the dark place in the shadows that concealed her. What was happening? Who was the duke searching for? She could not make sense of the conversation that she overheard, and she remained where she was, uncertain of what to do. She had wanted to push the letter under his door, or perhaps – if she was so adventurous –

place it inside his study on his desk, but now she dared not move. Something was happening, something unexpected and dreadful, and she did not know what it could be. Who could the duke be looking for? Who was gone? It could not be *herself*, or could it? She had barely been gone a few minutes and would have crossed paths with anyone who was looking for her.

Her eyes widened in surprise as she saw the duke emerge. His footsteps echoed in the cavernous hall as he strode past her, not seeing her. She watched as he mounted the stairs taking them two at a time. Where was he going, she wondered, her heart thumping and her pulse racing. Was he going to her room? With the letter still in her hand, she was overcome with curiosity and fear. This was all so unusual … She decided to abandon her task and raced to the stairwell after him. She ascended the steps as quickly as she could, her skirts raised above her ankles, not caring how ill-mannered that was, not at a time like this. Whatever was happening, she had never seen the duke in such a state, had never heard his voice sounding so forceful.

He moved quickly, but she was not far behind him. At the top of the stairs, she was astonished to see him burst into her room. What manner of situation could lead him to her chamber? Gasping from the run up the stairs, she rushed down the hall and towards her room to find a most shocking sight awaiting her. The Duke of Devonshire was standing in her room, in front of the trunk that lay open at the foot of the bed, her clothes packed neatly inside. He stood as though transfixed by what he was seeing, in his hand was a pair of her gloves that he lifted to his lips and then carefully, reverently placed in the trunk. She did not want to intrude upon him, and she did not understand what she was seeing, but she did know that he was treating her gloves with a gentleness, and affection that he had rarely shown her.

"Your Grace?" she whispered, her voice

barely audible as she stepped through the doorway.

In the dim glow of the candlelight, he turned towards her. She saw that her astonishment was matched by his own. He stepped towards her, his arms open as he said, "I thought you were gone."

"No," she said, aware of the letter in her hand and the open trunk in her room.

"I thought that I had lost you forever," he replied as he came closer.

Isabella did not answer. She watched him draw near and he touched her arms, his eyes fixed on hers, his expression softening as he spoke to her.

"The footman said that you had left – vanished. I could not believe it. I did not want to. Tell me that you are not leaving …"

"I have not yet left, but I intend to. Tomorrow…" she said as she let the words trail off and handed the letter to him.

He glanced at the letter. "What is this?"

"It will explain why I have to leave," she said as she felt the tears coming to her eyes.

"I shall open it right away." His hands began to open the letter.

"No, please, I would be embarrassed."

"You were not going to say goodbye?" he replied, hesitant to follow her request. Then he slid the letter into his coat pocket.

"I could not, I dared not," Isabella answered as she turned around, away from him. She could not look at him, not to say what she must. "I did not think that I mattered to you … You have done your duty, so I must go before I burden you for one more day and bring scandal upon your sister and your family. My half-brother has been found and arrested. He will surely hang for his crime … but it is more than that. The debt that you owed to my father has been discharged."

"A debt? You are not a debt," he said without hesitation, and she felt his presence, strong and masculine behind her.

"Yes, Your Grace, I *was* a debt and nothing

more. You owed my father a debt. That debt is no longer. So, I shall be gone, and you shall be absolved of all responsibility."

She felt his hands behind her on her shoulders and caught his masculine scent as he leaned close to her. She felt him against her back, the warmth of his body radiating through the thin material of her dress.

Did he kiss her hair? Did he hold her to him?

"You are more to me than a mere debt. If I have not offered you comfort or solace it is because I could not be near you, to be tempted by your wit ... and your nature ... your beauty ... I felt a regard that I have not felt for many years. That feeling grew stronger and frightened me with its strength, with the way I felt when I was near you. I could not permit myself to care for you, not when I knew I would lose you."

"I do not understand," she said as she slowly turned around, her mouth inches from his lips, her body against his, and she looked up at him. "Sir, you have given few indications that you care for me. I dared not to hope that the warmer gestures were nothing more than my heart's longing. You have spoken very little about my father, even though he was a dear friend to you. I felt that I faced the designs of my half-brother alone, and that you would not be able to conceal your association with me."

"Isabella, I did not abandon you," he whispered as he cupped her face with his hands. "I hired men to protect you as I searched for your half-brother. He was found in London through the efforts of my agents. We made fleeing impossible for him."

He paused, and in that moment, the relief that had briefly coursed through Isabella's veins slowed a little. She sensed that he was not yet finished with his story.

"There is something else of which my agents informed me. It seems possible that your half-brother has a child – however, we are still searching for the truth."

"A child?"

"Yes. I am sorry to say that the mother

seems to have allowed herself to be seduced away from her fiancé to be with your half-brother. Unfortunately, official records indicate that she died alone, giving birth to a daughter, shortly thereafter. What became of the abandoned child we do not know, yet. We have not located any child with your brother, and I do not have any more information, other than that, at present. Be assured, however, that we will not rest until we have established whether the child is safe and sound."

"How old is she?" Isabella asked. "What is her name?"

"I am afraid I do not yet have the answer."

"I am shocked, and I am so sorry…"

"Don't. The important thing is that your half-brother was arrested, and now you are safe and never have to fear again."

His words became softer. "It is I who should be sorry. When I think of how I behaved concerning your father, I am not proud. If I did not ask about your father, the hurt was too great. I wanted to remember him as I knew him. If I did not ask about you – that was done deliberately." He looked deep into her eyes. "I could not allow myself to fall in love with you – you, who must travel to London, to find a young man who was not tethered by memories and loss, as I am. I told myself that it was what you wanted, a gentleman who had not a care in the world, and who could give you a life of liberties and freedoms, not a life of tradition and convention." His face came closer to hers. "You changed me. You showed me that I could love again."

She broke away from him, tears falling down her face. "Why did you not tell me this? Why did you let me believe that I was a burden?"

"It was never my intention. However, I needed to be pragmatic. If you were a duty, I could distance myself from you. I could keep from loving you … I could let you go."

"Then let me go. Let me go now while I can. I never wanted to care for you, but now I will not be permitted to love you. My half-brother is arrested, and I am ruined. I bring nothing but scandal and disgrace. Let me leave, and we will speak nothing more of this."

"No, Isabella, you cannot leave. I do not care about the effect of any scandal concerning your half-brother, or the charges against him and his eventual punishment. It means little to me or my family, and I swear it will not taint you, as people will know you are innocent. I will see to it! But, I need you to remain at my side, you must stay. My gratitude to you is far deeper than you could possibly know for I have not told you everything. All you must have known of me was that I was saddened by a loss. I loved my wife, and I will always carry her memory in my heart, but I do not grieve any longer. She would not want that for me, she would wish for me to find happiness. With you, my dearest Isabella, I have found that happiness, that love that I thought was lost to me forever."

"I dare not," she said. "I care for your sister too much, for your family, for you." And she wept.

"Good Heavens, you must have heard. Have you not heard? Diana is missing!" The duchess appeared as Isabella was wiping her eyes.

"Lady Diana?" she gasped.

"She is gone!" the duchess exclaimed. "A footman saw a woman leave the residence with a man. He presumed it was you, Lady Isabella, but it was not. I was fearful of what to think, but Diana's maid has confirmed it. Diana has run away. The child has eloped!"

"Eloped?" The duke frowned.

"Her maid was sworn to secrecy, but she confessed. My daughter, my only daughter has run away with that dreadful baronet, the one I warned you about, Matthew! We must stop her before she is ruined!" the dowager duchess cried. "I cannot bear it. Oh, where is my maid? I must have tea to calm my nerves!"

The duchess left the bedroom abruptly. A silence fell between Isabella and the duke as he gazed into her eyes. "Isabella, I must go. I have to find my sister, but – not yet."

"You must leave – there is not time to talk if Lady Diana is in danger."

"I will," he said, his voice low and husky as he touched her face with his strong hands and caressed her cheeks gently. His eyes were sparkling in the light of a nearby candle, intoxicating her, as she breathlessly realised that she was helplessly in love. She loved him more than anything else in the world.

He kissed her, long and passionately. Their lips met as months of unspoken feelings, of misunderstandings, and of concealed emotions poured from them. Her arms were around his broad shoulders, and he pulled her instinctively towards him. He held her, kissed her until she was faint. Then, he kissed her forehead tenderly, as her eyes were still closed, and held her tightly to him.

Wordlessly, he left her, standing in the bedroom before her half-packed trunk, that she would no longer need. She opened her eyes and watched him leave. He stopped at the doorway and turned to her. He gazed at her. A tear fell down her cheek and then he was gone. His clean scent hung in the air around her, and her lips tingled.

LADY DIANA HAD BEEN FOUND at an inn, The Red Hart, not far from London. This was not to be confused with the infamous brothel that bore the same name and that was located right by the "Black Heart Tavern," a legendary boxing pub in Whitechapel – London's dark district. This one used by stagecoaches and carriages for the watering and resting of their horses and as lodging for weary travellers – particularly those travellers on their way to Gretna Green.

Unharmed and not ruined, she was tearfully returned to London, where it was revealed that she and Colonel Gardiner were in love. There was no doubting her love for him – it was clear that she adored him and always had.

For his part, Colonel Gardiner's motivations towards Isabella had been complex. Although he had initially admired Diana, the possibility of wooing and marrying the daughter of a duke had, at the time, seemed unattainable due to his lower rank (but as it turned out later, nonetheless, too much to resist), and he had turned his attentions towards Isabella. The fact that she was a highly attractive and intelligent companion had made it all the easier. However, he had eventually learned of her lack of a dowry, and the scandal that was tied to her. He was also not foolish, and the evening at the ball had confirmed his suspicions that she and the duke were nurturing a growing regard for each other.

It was possible he realised this even before they acknowledged it to one another.

In the end his plans were foiled.

So, upon learning of Isabella's unsuitability, he chose – rather boldly – to return to the pursuit of his first and (as he quickly realised beforehand by his frequent visits to see *both* women at the manor) true love, Lady Diana. They had planned to be married before anyone could object to it, yet, the duke and his men, and mostly the dowager duchess had done just that. However, the impediment was temporary, as Lady Diana managed to win her prize – the baronet Colonel Gardiner – with many tears and much cajoling.

Summer returned to Hardwick Manor, and with it, the Danvers family. This time, there was an unexpected addition (to the dowager duchess's dismay) to the family – Colonel Gardiner. In the weeks leading up to the wedding, Isabella assisted Lady Diana in planning her dress for the special day. The young bride chose a light-blue ribbon for her bonnet and for her bouquet. The ribbon was of an identical hue to the one that Isabella remembered well — the length of blue ribbon that she had discovered in the garden that late autumn afternoon. She thought again about the barely glimpsed hint of a crimson uniform, and asked Diana about it that afternoon.

"Diana, I know you meant no harm or scandal to come from it, but I have to ask you –

did you perchance meet the colonel in the garden of the manor at the end of the summer?"

Diana reddened but quickly replied, "I did, Isabella. He sent word that he wished to speak with me in private, and I saw no harm in meeting him in the walled garden near the house. I thought that no one would see us, and that I would still be close to home and safety. I know it was foolish of me. But how did you know?"

"I suspected it when you chose this blue ribbon," her friend replied. I found one just like it caught in the bushes of the garden that evening."

"Oh, I gave it to the colonel as a token of my affection," Diana said. "If he lost it, I imagine he did not wish to hurt my feelings by telling me of his carelessness." She smiled cheerfully.

Isabella could well imagine him accidently letting it slip from his grasp in the windy autumn evening as he hastily left the garden. Perhaps he had heard her approach, and in his haste to exit and not be caught, he had lost his love-token.

No matter the true circumstances, it had been a romantic gesture that she now understood. This simple act gave Isabella reason to believe that all would be well with the couple, despite their vast difference in rank and the tumultuous beginning to their union.

"I must admit, Diana, I have been blind for far too long and did not realise that you were so fond of him." Isabella searched her dear friend's eyes. "Although, you did speak of him with much enthusiasm each time a conversation came about."

"I presume I was rather obvious, perhaps only in your company. He grew on me over time. I do hope you are not bothered by my behaviour."

Isabella placed her hands on Diana's shoulders and smiled. "Not at all! There is nothing to forgive. Why would I ever be upset or bothered by your happiness? You are so very dear to me.

I wish you a *lifetime* of love! This is a most joyous occasion."

She was not alone in her hopes for dear Lady Diana, as evidenced by the many visitors to Hardwick Manor, who wished the young woman good fortune and a happy life with her baronet.

Two months after this conversation, Lady Diana was married to Colonel Gardiner, ecstatically (and with a *greatly* reduced dowry), in a modest ceremony at Beyton Dale. The ceremony brought much joy to the village and to the Prices, who professed themselves not at all surprised by the turn of events. The pair was gifted in the art of village gossip and had suspected all along that Lady Diana and a certain baronet were in love. As did Mary, Isabella's loyal maid who Isabella suspected had heard about the couple in the servants' hall.

The dowager duchess, Lady Diana's mother, had been unable to calm at first, blaming the baronet for charming her daughter away. However, she quickly learned that Diana had had her own part to play in the intrigue. The baronet's own willingness to confess his mistakes to make amends meant such, but she slowly began to accept him as a son-in-law, especially, once she saw that he truly made Diana happy.

The fact that her own son had finally found happiness after so many years had the largest effect on the dowager duchess's change of heart.

*D*iana's was not the only wedding to cause a stir in Beyton Dale that summer. A second, far more lavish ceremony than any before it in the history of the little village, was witnessed by a great many guests at the church. It was a wedding that would be talked about for months afterwards, because it celebrated the union of a duke and his lovely bride. The brown-haired beauty, whom the locals had previously known as a tragic figure, was no longer dressed in the sombre colours of mourning. She was now a welcome and fashionable addition to Derbyshire and the local gentry.

The anticipated scandal of Isabella's half-brother's trial and conviction had been smaller than she could have imagined. As a viscount, he had been quietly tried and sentenced to transportation to Australia for his crimes, never to return. As his less influential sister, she had barely been mentioned in the newspaper reports, which preferred to wallow in her half-brother's shocking lack of affection for his father. And afterwards, as the new Duchess of Devonshire, she had become someone else – someone new – and from that point on, she did not figure into the story at all.

Furthermore, a new Earl of Chatham had taken Isabella's father's place, a distant cousin, and a gentleman she had never met. She did not begrudge the heir his due, not when she was so deliriously happy herself.

After some impressive detective work, and several judicious payments of money, Mr Hayworth had been able to locate the child of

Charles Thornton and his deceased lover, four-year-old Emma, who was being cared for by various acquaintances of her mother.

Matthew and Isabella had decided to take Emma in. Isabella knew all too well how a loving parent could buffer one from the sorrows of life, and she also knew the loneliness and isolation of losing that love and of being dependent upon others. For his own part, Matthew was grateful that he had been granted a second chance at happiness, and he readily agreed to offer the child a second chance at having the warmth, care, and love a family provided.

The child's arrival was eagerly anticipated by all at Hardwick Manor, almost the same as it had been when they were awaiting Isabella's arrival, all those months ago. There was one difference this time – there was no fear *or* hesitation.

At last, the happy day arrived, and she stood before them in a pink dress and a straw hat, with a big pink bow to match, a doll in her hand. From that moment on, Emma had filled their home with sunshine and laughter.

ALMOST ONE YEAR later to the day, on a fine evening, Isabella walked with Matthew out into the gardens.

The weddings and the scandals, like the last of the summer blooms, were already gone, turned to memories when the autumn moon cast its light upon a beautiful young woman in the garden of the great residence. She appeared as ethereal in the moon's beams as she had that first night she arrived at Hardwick Manor. Looking up at the stars overhead, Isabella reflected upon recent events and realised, once again, that she was truly fortunate.

"Isabella, there is a chill to the air, shall we go inside?" the Duke of Devonshire said as he wrapped his coat around her shoulders.

She loved the smell of him that lingered on his clothes, and that enveloped her as she felt the warmth from his body still clinging to the material of his coat.

"No, not yet. Perhaps this is the last beautiful night we will have before the cold winter sets in. Let us enjoy our walk in the garden."

"A good idea, my dearest Isabella," he replied as he reached for her hand.

She looked down at her small hand in his as they strolled along the path to the arbour. The evening breeze blew gently through the branches of the trees overhead and stirred the leaves under their feet. She was happy, completely, and totally happy ... and she knew that she would not be alone in her happiness, not for long.

She squeezed his hand and spoke the words that she knew would complete his happiness. "Matthew, I have something to tell you." She gazed up at the man she loved, her husband. "Something that will change our lives, even more so than it has changed this past year."

He stopped, turned to her, and held her close to him. He looked into her eyes and was captivated by the glistening moonlight he saw in them. "You have changed my life, Isabella. You have made me happy beyond measure … I have no right to ask for more."

"You have every right to ask for more, for an heir. Matthew, you are going to be a father again. I am expecting a child."

He did not speak – he only stared at her.

His heart welled with a joy he scarcely imagined he could feel.

As he kissed her lips, his passion and love for her surged deep within him, and he could not imagine being a happier man than he was on that autumn night. As he kissed her again and again, her laughter joined his as they planned their future. They spoke of their children, and of their growing family. They could not know that they were the same as many couples both before and after them, intoxicated with the joy of bringing a new life into the world. And several months later, that new life, little Alexander, was delivered safely to a future as the next Duke of Devonshire.

Walking hand in hand under the stars, as leaves fell from the trees and swirled all around them, the duke and his unexpected bride were both completely happy.

The End

BOOKS IN THE SAME SERIES

The Wharton Series:

A Bride for the Viscount's Cold Son

Large Print Edition ISBN: 1705473342

The Duke of the Moors

Large Print Edition ISBN: 1654985503

An Orphan for the Duke

Large Print Edition ISBN: 9798632901741

All Books can be read as standalones.

More Large Print Editions coming soon!

For more details, visit:

www.audreyashwood.com/large-print

ABOUT THE AUTHOR

Audrey Ashwood

Author of Sweet Historical Romance

Audrey Ashwood hails from London, the city where she was born and raised. At a young age, she began diving into the world of literature, a world full of fairytales and Prince Charmings. Writing came later – no longer was she a spectator of fantasies; she was now a creator of them.

In her books, the villains get their just desserts – her stories are known for happy and deserved endings. Love, of course, plays a major role, even if it's not the initial star of the show. With each written word, Audrey hopes to remind people that love transcends oceans and generations.

Don't miss out on exciting offers and new releases.
Sign up for her newsletter:
www.audreyashwood.com/releases

Find Audrey Ashwood on Amazon:
www.amazon.com/author/audreyashwood

An Orphan for the Duke (Large Print Edition V3);

A Regency Romance Novel by Audrey Ashwood;

Published by:

ARP 5519, 1732 1st Ave #25519 New York, NY 10128

Contact: info@allromancepublishing.com

Large Print Edition (Version 3.0); July 9th, 2020

Image Rights: Depositphotos.com

Illustrations and Cover: ARP Cover Design

Printed in Great Britain
by Amazon